SN

Helen Cresswell was born in Nottinghamshire, the middle child of three. She started writing poems and stories at the age of six and has not stopped since. She has had a varied and successful career since leaving university, during which time she has been a literary assistant, a teacher, and worked prolifically for BBC television. She is the popular author of *many* stories for children and adults and has been in print for 35 years.

Helen has two grown-up daughters and two granddaughters, and lives in an old farmhouse in Nottinghamshire.

*Also published by Helen Cresswell and available from
Hodder Children's Books*

Bag of Bones
The Night-watchmen

The Bagthorpe Saga
Ordinary Jack
Absolute Zero
Bagthorpes Unlimited
Bagthorpes v. the World
Bagthorpes Abroad
Bagthorpes Haunted
Bagthorpes Liberated

And for younger readers:
The Little Sea Horse
The Sea Piper
The Little Grey Donkey
A Game of Catch
The Winklesea Trilogy

SNATCHERS

Helen Cresswell

a division of Hodder Headline plc

First published in Great Britain in 1998
by Hodder Children's Books

This paperback edition published in Great Britain in 1999
by Hodder Children's Books

A Catalogue record for this book is
available from the British Library

ISBN 0 340 68287 6

Typeset by Hewer Text Ltd, Edinburgh
Printed and bound in Great Britain by
Clays Ltd, St Ives Plc

Hodder Children's Books
A Division of Hodder Headline
338 Euston Road
London NW1 3BH

For Ellie

BEFORE YOU BEGIN . . .

Listen, I have a story to tell. It's mad and sad in parts and beautiful as well. Most stories have a time and a place. They happen because a particular person was in a particular place at a particular time. Think about it. If Wendy Darling had not lived in a certain tall house in a certain street in London, we should never have known the story of Peter Pan.

The particular person in this story is called Ellie. But I don't know when it happened, or where. It wasn't anywhere and it wasn't any time. It wasn't last year, I think, or the year before that. And as to where it happened – your guess is as good as mine. Some might say that in that case it never happened at all, anywhere. But I say it did happen, somewhere.

How do I know? Well, if you look at the moon long enough you can soon begin to see a face, and the next thing you know you have a man in the moon. But if *you* look at the moon, you see one face. If *I* look at it, I see another. And that's the way it is with stories. They are there in your head, hidden in a kind of fog, and then, bit by bit, you begin to see them happening.

At first you see only snatches, glimpses. I saw a snowy street and then I saw a wolf woman with yellow teeth and then – ppffff! They'd gone. A cloud had gone over the moon. The next thing I saw was a raggedy boy with spiky hair and popping eyes. Who was he, and where did he come from?

And so it went on, for days and weeks and months and years. For all I know, this story has been making itself since the day I was born (and that is a very long time ago). Because that is what stories do, they make themselves. Or rather, they grow.

If ever you have planted a seed in a pot you'll know how mysterious it was. All you have to do is remember to water it and then, secretly and amazingly, it begins to stir down there in the dark. You wait and wait until suddenly, from one day to the next, there's a tiny shoot of green showing above the soil. And it will grow into whatever it is meant to be. You can't do anything about it. You can't make a parsley seed grow a poppy, and a forget-me-not can't turn into a sunflower. (Sunflower seeds are the best to grow. In one short summer they grow and grow until they're taller than you are, and that's a very strange feeling. Try it.)

I hope this story is a sunflower. I don't know yet, because it isn't finished. It might turn out not to be suitable for children at all. A real nasty. I hope not. You and I will discover together. We know already that there will be a snowy street and a wolf woman and a boy with spiky hair. I know a few other things, too, and will tell you them when they happen . . .

ONE

THE BEGINNING OF THINGS

We must begin at the beginning with this girl called Ellie. She was pale and skinny and had big round eyes, all the better to stare with. She was born one January night when the north wind was blowing snow and rattling all the windows of the town. She came into the world with a kind of long shout, as if she were glad to be there. The nurses were surprised. Usually they had to turn babies upside down and smack them to get the first cry out.

The baby was wrapped up tightly and propped in the crook of her mother's arm. Her mother gazed down and thought this was the most beautiful baby there had ever been. She wasn't, of course. That is what all mothers think. Most new babies aren't beautiful at all. They're squashed and wrinkled and look cross – as they probably are. It's a long hard journey to get into the world (and a long hard journey when you get there, as Ellie would discover).

Usually babies don't have adventures. They suck and sleep and sleep and suck, and in between they have their nappies changed. Not much of a story there.

And Ellie wasn't christened, so there's no story there, either. No good fairies giving her beauty and wisdom and so forth, and no bad fairy to send her to sleep for a hundred years. (And anyway, that story's already been told.)

On the other hand, you couldn't help feeling that some kind of fate was wished for Ellie, because of what happened. There are some people who go through life without anything much happening to them at all. And there are others who seem to throw off sparks and crackle like electricity. They are magnets, and wild and wonderful and terrible things come flying to them one after another in a storm.

That's how Ellie was, right from the beginning. The first thing happened when she was only a few months old.

Mrs Horner had put her baby out in the garden

to sleep, and went back inside to make a pie. It was lucky that she was in the kitchen or she might never have seen her daughter again. She was up to her elbows in flour when she happened to glance out of the window. What she saw made her squeak. What she saw was a tall dark woman going swiftly over the grass towards Ellie's pram.

Mrs Horner ran straight out, and by the time she got there the woman had already snatched the baby from the pram.

'No! No!' screamed Mrs Horner, and tried to take her baby back.

The two women struggled and pulled, and by now Ellie was bawling, and who knows what would have happened if at that very moment a large dog had not run up, and started to growl and snap at the stranger's heels.

'And that was the strangest thing,' Mrs Horner would tell her daughter as she grew up. 'I'd never seen that dog before in my life! And the minute that woman ran off he ran after her, and we never saw him again!'

Ellie loved stories, and this was her favourite of all.

'Tell me what he looked like!' she begged.

'Oooh, ever so big, with a thick coat and golden eyes and sharp ears!'

'A wolf,' nodded Ellie. 'It was a wolf. And did he save me?'

'Oh yes,' her mother said. 'That terrible woman was bigger than me, and stronger.'

'A witch!' Ellie said. 'Like the witch in *Rapunzel*. Did she have a cloak and a pointy hat?'

Ellie knew perfectly well that she didn't. She had heard the story a hundred times before, but still hoped that her would-be kidnapper would turn out to be a witch.

'And then you ran back in the house!'

'I did!'

'And you put me down on the draining board and locked the back door, and then you ran and locked the front door.'

'Oh I did, I can tell you!'

'And then you rang the police and went back in the kitchen — and where was I?'

'You'd slid down the draining board and into the sink, and there you were in the soapy water with all the cups and saucers!'

'Splashing about, I was, and laughing!'

'And soap suds flying everywhere! I just scooped you out and—'

'—and I was sopping wet and I wetted you all over and then the police came and we lived happily ever after!'

'Something like that,' said her mother.

Two

A BROKEN PROMISE

Mrs Horner was so pleased with her baby that she decided to have another. Not straight away, though.

'We'll wait until Ellie starts school,' she told her husband.

So they did. But you can't just order a baby like a bunch of flowers or a new carpet. By the time one did come along Ellie was already in the third class at school. This new baby was a boy called Sam and needless to say was the most beautiful baby there had ever been. Even Ellie thought so, at first. She would stare at him for hours on end and he'd stare back and say 'Coo! coo!' and curl his tiny fingers and toes.

But he grew up to be quite a terror, and by the time he was two would scream and stamp till his face was scarlet and tears gushed down his fat cheeks. Ellie honestly thought he might explode.

15

She even wished he would sometimes. Mrs Horner didn't seem very worried about having a monster in the family.

'You were just the same at that age,' she told Ellie (who did not believe it, not likely).

Sam took so long coming that for seven years Ellie was an only child, and behaved like one. She read a lot of books and daydreamed and played secret games with imaginary friends. She had a whole world of her own inside her head.

It was one perfectly ordinary day in September when it happened. Ellie had just bought a bag of plums. They were plump and golden and the juice dribbled down her chin. She sat on the wooden seat outside the library, and as she finished each plum she spat the stone to see how far it would go.

One or two people frowned at her, though she couldn't see why. She was spitting plum stones. Nothing the matter with that. With any luck, one day the library would stand in an orchard.

'Give us one!' said a voice.

Ellie turned and saw a boy of about her own age. He was rather raggedy, and had spiky hair and strange, liquid eyes.

'Who're you?' she demanded. 'Never seen you before.'

'Never mind,' he said. 'Give us a plum. Go on.'

'You don't go to my school.'

'Don't go to any school.'

'That's nice,' Ellie said. 'If it was true.'

'It is true,' the boy said.

'Must have a funny mum and dad, if they don't make you go to school.'

'Haven't got a mum and dad.'

'What? You must have.'

'Haven't.'

'Have.'

'Haven't.'

'Look,' Ellie said, 'everyone in the whole world's got a mum and dad. Don't you know anything? Don't you know how babies get born?'

She did. Your mum and dad made you, and you came out of your mother's belly button.

'P'raps you don't know who they are,' she said kindly. 'Are you an orphan?'

'No,' said the boy. 'If you must know, I'm an angel.'

17

'You must think I'm daft,' Ellie said. 'You're nothing like one. Where're your wings?'

'Lost 'em,' the boy said. He sounded sad, as if he really once *had* had wings, and had lost them.

'Mine are tucked flat under my sweater,' Ellie told him. 'I don't use them a lot. And my spare pair's being washed.'

'Are you going to give me a plum or what?'

'OK.' She offered him the bag, and he took one.

To Ellie's surprise, he didn't eat it. He just squashed it between finger and thumb. From the pulpy mess he took out the stone.

'Funny way to eat a plum,' Ellie said.

He let the juicy flesh drop from his fingers, then licked them clean.

'Bet I can spit farther than you!' he said.

'Bet you can't!'

He spat. The stone flew from his mouth. It rose into the air in a smooth arc – and stayed there. Ellie stared. The stone hovered like a kestrel.

'I could make it go a hundred miles if I wanted,' the boy said.

'What's happening? Why doesn't it fall?'

She didn't like it. A plum stone was bobbing in midair in broad daylight outside the library.

'Make it fall!' she commanded.

'OK. Farther than any of yours though. Easy peasy.'

The stone started to fall, but not straight down. It sailed on and fell a good metre farther than Ellie's best spit so far.

'That'll be a tree one day,' he said smugly. 'A great big pink cherry!'

'Plum, you mean.'

He shrugged.

'What's the difference?'

'It's a plum stone. It's got to be a plum tree.'

'Look,' he said, 'I think you're forgetting. I'm an angel. Do anything, I can. If I want that plum stone to grow into a dirty great oak tree, it will.'

'And pigs might fly!' Ellie said.

'Bet you!' he said.

It seemed a safe enough bet. Even if he was right, oaks took years to grow. Hundreds of years.

'OK.' Ellie told him. 'Bet you . . . bet you . . .'

'Your bike!' the boy said.

'How d'you know I've got one?'

19

'Oh, I know,' he told her.

Ellie hesitated. She loved her bike. Besides, imagine the trouble she'd get into.

'What're you betting me?' she countered.

The angel (if that is what he was) looked at her thoughtfully.

'I bet you,' he said, 'a real pair of wings.'

'*What?*'

Ellie was all at once dizzy. She'd be able to fly like a bird – she'd always wanted to. It was what she pretended to be doing half the time when she was on her bike.

'Hang on,' she said. '*You* haven't got real wings, and you're supposed to be an angel. If you can just wish for them, why don't you get a pair of your own?'

'Don't know anything about angels, do you?' he said. 'The whole point of angels is that they do things for other people. Don't worry, I can get you wings, all right. P'raps not straightaway, though. You might have to wait a bit. Pity you can't get me some.'

He sounded sad again. Ellie was beginning to believe him.

'OK,' she said. 'Wings.'

'That I can't make that plum stone grow into an oak?'

She nodded. She knew he couldn't win. It would be years before the stone would be even a sapling.

He grinned.

'Here goes!'

They both looked over to where the stone had landed.

It happened so quickly that Ellie did not see the actual moment when the stone must have put out its first roots and started to grow. She only knew that it did, because there it was – first a sprout, then a sapling, then a tree. And one moment it was bare, then it had buds, then golden leaves. It was spinning through the seasons and Ellie's head went spinning with it.

The tree was already higher than the roof before she managed to croak a single word.

'Stop!'

Spring, summer, autumn, winter. Spring, summer, autumn, winter.

'Stop! Please! Oh stop!'

'I win?'

'You win.'

The tree stopped growing. It settled into the September day with a shiver of leaves already turning gold. It was an oak.

'Oh help!' said Ellie faintly.

She was so shocked that she wondered if her hair had turned white. And what if – she looked down at her hands and saw with relief that they were still her own, and recognisable. If she too had gone spinning through the seasons, by now they would be wrinkled and spotted brown. By now she would be old. Ancient.

'Now what?' the boy asked. 'Want me to turn it back, or leave it?'

Ellie had not thought of that. She glanced round quickly. There were the usual Saturday-morning shoppers. Not one of them seemed to notice that an oak had sprung up, even though it was lit like a lamp in the sunlight on the dusty road. They would though, sooner or later, she thought. And Mrs Flynn in the library, she'd notice, bound to.

On the other hand, no one would know why. No one would connect it with her, Ellie

Horner. Why should they? And the world needed more trees.

'Leave it,' she decided. 'Might as well.'

So he did. And in the end, of course, people did notice, and all kinds of questions were asked. Letters were written to *The Times* and clever men from universities came to look at the tree. But that was later, much later. What we want to know is what happened to Ellie next.

THREE

CONSEQUENCES

For a start, there was a bet to settle. Ellie wished she could get out of it.

'It wasn't fair,' she said.

'Why not?'

'Because you knew you'd win, that's why. Real bets are on things that might happen and might not.'

'You knew *you'd* win,' the boy told her. 'Go on – admit it.'

Ellie did not reply. It was true. She *had* known she'd win. Everyone knows oak trees can't grow from plum stones, not even in a month of Sundays, let alone a few seconds.

'I'll tell you one thing that's funny,' she said after a while.

'What?'

'Nobody even seems to notice that tree.'

'So?'

24

'P'raps it's not there. Not really. Perhaps I only *think* it's there.'

'Same difference,' the boy said.

'It's not! And perhaps I only think you're an angel because you told me so!'

'I am,' he said.

'No halo, no wings, and where's your harp?'

The boy looked at her long and hard. His eyes were strange, they were round like marbles. Sometimes they were greeny-blue like the sea and sometimes almost silvery. Looking into them made Ellie dizzy.

'Show us your belly button!' he commanded.

'*What*?'

'Go on – show us!'

She was shocked. She had only known this boy five minutes. You have to know people a lot longer than that before you show them your bare tum.

'Not likely,' she said at last.

'You have got one?'

''Course I have. Everyone has. It's how you get born.'

He did not reply. Instead, he lifted his shirt

25

and showed his middle, his bare, white, smooth middle.

Ellie gasped.

'It's – it's lower down! It must be lower down!'

For reply he tugged at the waist of his pants. Smooth, white and without a pucker.

Ellie started to feel dizzy again.

'*Now* do you believe me?'

At any moment Ellie expected a pig to fly past. Everyone has a belly button. Her mother and father had, and Sam, and everyone in her class. You needed one to get born. So if this boy hadn't got one, he couldn't have been born. So in that case . . .

'I think I'll go home now,' she said, and started to walk.

'Wait! No! Don't go!'

Ellie kept walking. She was walking away from the impossible oak and the even more impossible boy. If she wanted a fairy tale, she'd get one from the library.

'The bike! You said I could have your bike!'

It was a mean thing she was doing, a rotten

mean thing, and she knew it. She was walking away from a promise.

'I'm going to pretend the whole thing never happened,' she told herself. 'It probably didn't, anyway.'

The trouble was, it had. No matter how hard she tried to bury herself in ordinariness, it didn't work. For dinner it was sausages and chips. Ellie daubed them with ketchup and wondered what the boy was having for his dinner. He was a lost angel without wings in a strange town.

She tried to picture him in McDonald's, but couldn't. In any case, probably angels were like the Queen and didn't carry money. He probably doesn't get hungry, she told herself. People without belly buttons probably don't. He never ate that plum. Probably he doesn't eat at all.

There were too many probablys.

'Mum,' she asked, 'does *everyone* have a belly button?'

'That's a funny question to come up with at dinner-time.'

'But do they?'

'Of course they do. They couldn't have been born otherwise.'

That was exactly what Ellie was afraid of.

She decided again to forget the whole thing. But that's impossible as everyone knows. The more you try to forget something, the more it comes bobbing into your mind. Just as the harder you try to remember something, the more unlikely it is that you will. Your mind is a funny thing. It seems to have a mind of its own. It must have, if you think about it.

When you go to bed and put your head on the pillow and shut your eyes, you can't think 'Now, what shall I dream tonight? I know, I'll dream that school changes into an ice-cream factory, and I'm in charge! Or shall I dream that I'm a wolf, then everyone I don't like can be my dinner!'

No. A dream isn't like a video that you can pick off a shelf. You don't choose your dreams, they choose you. Spooky.

Anyway, Ellie might want to forget all about the boy and the promise, but part of her mind didn't – or couldn't. The sun went in and a chill wind blew through the town and Ellie shivered and wondered if it were anything to do with her. She wondered if leaves were being blown from the brand new oak. She wanted to go and look, but didn't dare. She tried to forget about that, too, but couldn't. It was there, like an itch she could not scratch.

Nothing she did could help. She went to her room, but it didn't feel as if it were hers any more. It was as if she were a visitor. She stared round at her toys and games and thought how dull and pointless they were, what silly things.

A jigsaw lay half-finished on the table by the window. She went over to slot in a few more pieces. She didn't have much luck, though. Somehow the colours were blurred and wishy-washy, and her eyes couldn't seem to pick them out.

Come on, Ellie, she told herself. You're a whizz at jigsaws, everybody says so.

All the time it was getting darker, and now the windows were rattling and the cold wind was right inside the room. It moaned and lifted papers, it made the light swing on its cord and the curtains billow.

Nothing like it had ever happened before, and Ellie tried to pretend it wasn't happening now. If you ignore things they usually go away in the end. She sat on her bed and picked up a book, which is as good a way as any to escape from the world.

It didn't work. She stared at the page but the words were just a jumble of letters, they didn't make sense. The wind kept gusting and blowing the pages and now she was cold, very cold. It was mid-afternoon, but nearly dark, and still she had the feeling that it was something to do with her. She even wondered if it was only her house that the wind and darkness were visiting, and whether the town was still flooded with sunlight in a perfectly ordinary September day.

She could not go and look because of the boy, and the tree. She was stuck here in the windy darkness in a place that didn't even seem like home any more. Half-fearfully she looked around her and tried to remind herself that this was her home, and these were her own dear, familiar things, and she was safe.

Safe as houses.

She had no sooner thought it than an icy draught went by and brushed her skin into goosebumps and plucked the book right out of her hands. She saw it go sailing across the room and drop somewhere in the dimness. It was impossible, but she saw it happen.

She turned to see whether the window had blown open, but it hadn't. She caught sight of something in the garden, and what she saw was another impossible thing.

Four

KIDNAP

Under the apple tree was a pram. Ellie recognised it even in the gloom. It was her pram, the one her mother had kept for seven years to be Sam's. The pram her father had sold only last month at a car boot sale. The pram they didn't have any more.

Ellie shook her head and shut her eyes, then opened them again. She watched what happened next as if it were a film with the sound turned down. The tall shape of a woman was advancing swiftly over the grass, and it was no one Ellie had ever seen before, and yet she seemed to recognise her. She was filled with a huge dread. The woman bent over the pram and snatched up a baby and turned to go.

'The dog! Where's the dog?'

The woman was going now, the baby in her arms, as swiftly as she had come.

'No! No!'

Ellie screamed and battered the glass with her fists. She was being kidnapped, just as in the old story, but the story was going wrong. There was meant to be a dog, and her mother was meant to come running from the house. They were all meant to live happily ever after.

'I've gone!' she whispered at last.

It was horrible. It was a nightmare. Ellie went like a sleep-walker over to her bed and picked up the old rag doll and started to suck its fingers.

It didn't have fingers, actually. It never did have, but even if it had they would have been sucked away long before now. Mrs Horner had had to keep stitching up the ends of its arms to keep the stuffing from coming out. The doll was called Moppet, but Mrs Horner called it Ellie's Little Comfort, and often said she felt like throwing it into the dustbin.

When Ellie was tiny, once she had stopped sucking her thumb she had started sucking the doll instead. It made her feel safe and happy. She didn't do it so much these days, but if there was ever a time when she needed comfort, it was now.

Suck suck suck.

She could hardly think, but even when she did,
the thoughts she had were bad.

It was me that woman took.

Suck suck suck

There was meant to be a big dog to
save me.

Suck suck suck

If that was me, perhaps I'm not really
here at all now.

Suck suck suck

It's dark and windy and I think the end
of the world's coming.

Suck suck suck

Suck suck suck

Ellie thought that perhaps it was only her house
the wind and darkness were visiting, but she was
wrong. Out there in the town leaves were blowing
up the High Street in a storm, and the cars were
crawling with their headlamps on. The people were
frightened.

'It's not natural!'

They stared up at the sky, which was navy blue
with yellowy streaks.

Old people hurried back home and slammed their doors and locked them. Mothers kept tight hold of their children's hands. Groups of men stood on corners while the leaves blew past them, and had to shout above the howl of the wind.

'What's going on?'

'I blame it on the government!'

No one noticed a tall dark woman with a baby in her arms and a thin smile on her lips. She kept striding, striding, and if the baby was crying no one heard it above the racket of the wind. The whole town was shaking, the doors and windows rattled.

'Whee! Wheee! Lift off!' yelled a gang of kids.

No one noticed a small boy hunched in a doorway. His face was white and shocked and his eyes were popping.

'Oh no! Oh no!' he whispered, and the words were blown back into his mouth.

No one noticed that there were strangers about. They went in pairs and wore dark glasses. They were men with hats and long raincoats with the collars turned up. They looked like gangsters in an old movie.

No one noticed that their hats did not blow off in the gale. Other hats were flying everywhere, mixed in with the leaves. Hats with feathers and hats with brims and old ladies' hats of felt and fur. People chased after them but could not catch them. They were bowled along by the rude wind and would go on blowing right out of town.

The tall men in raincoats were not invisible. Each had a leather wallet and in it was a photograph of a boy. They stopped people as they came out of shops and showed them the photo.

'Have you seen this boy?'

'This boy's gone missing – have you seen him?'

'There's a reward.'

The woman with the baby went on striding, striding with her face to the wind. Now the baby was crying but no one heard it above the din, and in any case, babies cry all the time. Nobody bothered to look at the woman, either. If they had, they might have been scared. They might even have put two and two together, and guessed that she had come visiting along with the doomy wind and darkness.

Her lips were drawn back in a kind of snarl and her teeth were yellowy and pointed, and what she looked like was a wolf. She wore a long black coat, but maybe that was to disguise the length of her spine, the shortness of her legs. It did not do to look too closely at her hands and feet. One pair was covered by mittens, the other by shoes that were curiously narrow and small. There did not seem to be room in them for fingers and toes.

She turned a corner and almost ran into a man with his dog.

'Whoops!' cried the man. 'Sorry, madam! What a wind, what a wind! Jason, down!'

The dog stiffened and growled, deep down in its throat. It made a spring that almost pulled its owner off his feet.

'Jason, down!' he bawled into the wind.

The woman twitched her coat and wheeled clear of the straining animal and was on her way again.

'Jason, *heel*!' said the man. 'Rum-looking woman, that – and was it a *baby* she was carrying?'

And that was the nearest anybody came to sussing the kidnapper.

The cats of the town did, though. Blown sideways

by the wind and fur on end, they arched and spat as the woman went by. Tortoiseshell, black, ginger and tabby, they crouched on walls or lurked in alleys, and when they caught the scent of the woman they stiffened and hissed like wild things. Their owners would never have recognised their tame little Kitts and Topsys.

The woman turned another corner and was in a street of terraced houses, of red bricks with blue slate roofs, alike as peas in pods. At number thirteen she stopped. (There was no number thirteen in that street, and never had been.)

With her free hand she lifted the knocker. Rat tat tat! Rat tat tat! Still the wind blew and still the baby cried.

The door opened and the woman slipped inside and the door closed again behind her.

All at once it was amazingly quiet and still. There was not the least sound of the wind still funnelling up the street outside. It was as if she were in another place – or time – or both.

'I'm back, Boss,' she said.

FIVE

INVISIBLE

Ellie had sucked and sucked at the rag doll till the end of its arm was flat and soggy. The sucking comforted her, as it always had.

I've been stolen.

I've got to do something about it.

Suck suck suck

I'll have to go and find myself and get myself back.

Suck suck suck

That angel – he'll help me!

Suck suck suck

But I broke my promise!

Suck suck suck suck suck suck

I can *un*break it!

She stared out. Beyond the glass she could see the inky sky and madly shaking trees. It was nearly as dark as night, and Ellie was afraid of the dark, and always had been. It was a prowling monster that might swallow her whole

39

And this was no ordinary dark. It had blown in on a howling gale. It was alive, almost. She was more scared than she had ever been in her life before, and more alone. She had been stolen from her pram by a stranger, and there was no one she could tell.

But if I really *was* stolen, why am I here now?

Suck suck suck

Am I here now?

Suck suck suck suck suck suck

Bang bang bang.

She could hear her own heart beating in her ears. There, above the chest of drawers, was the mirror. It glinted darkly in the gloom.

Ellie stared at it for a long, long time. Then, slowly, she stood up, but still clutched the doll, because if ever she needed comfort it was now.

Am I here?

Am I . . . ?

There's only one way to find out, Ellie Horner. The trouble with life is that things come piling one on top of another. You thought things were bad, but if you look in that glass and don't see yourself looking back, they'll get worse.

Much worse.

I'll just have one last suck.

Suck suck suck suck suck suck suck suck.

Suck suck suck suck.

Now!

She stepped forward and looked into the mirror.

EEEEEEEECH!

Her scream mingled horribly, with the howl of the wind. She turned and fled. She ran downstairs.

'Help! Help! Help!'

Mr Horner was watching football on television. Mrs Horner was helping Sam to build his farmyard. The lights were all switched on, and Ellie blinked in the sudden brightness.

'I've never known anything like it!' Mrs Horner was saying. 'Black as night and such a wind – it won't blow the roof off, I hope.'

'Mum! Dad! Look at me!'

'Funny, that,' said Mr Horner, without taking his eyes off the screen. 'This match is only twenty miles up the road and look – the sun's shining.'

'It must be a weather pocket,' said Mrs Horner wisely.

Ellie's own scream was still ringing in her ears. She tried again.

'Mum! Dad!'

She wanted them to prove the mirror wrong.

'Big big castle!' said Sam happily.

'It's me – Ellie!'

'I'll put the kettle on.' Mrs Horner stood up and moved forward and Ellie had to sidestep smartly.

'Ellie!' her mother called. 'Ellie, come down, I want you!'

'I'm *here*! Are you blind? Are you deaf?'

'Goodness knows what she finds to do up there.'

'There's a woman been and stolen me from my pram!'

The doors and windows rattled in a mighty gust that seemed to rock the house.

'Please!' Ellie was sobbing now. 'Please look at me! Tell me I'm here!'

'Always been a lot on her own, of course,' Mrs

Horner was saying. 'With being an only for so long, I expect.'

I'm an only now, thought Ellie. *Worse* than an only.

She tasted salt on her lips. She didn't even wait to snatch up a jacket, she ran to the door, opened it and went out. The wind blew in and Mr Horner's newspaper went flapping off along the carpet as if it were alive. Mrs Horner screamed.

'What was that?'

'Ay, what was it?'

'The door opened and then shut and there's no one there!'

It was a bad moment for them, but it was even worse for Ellie. What could have got into her – why was she now outside in the windy darkness when she could still have been safe inside, at home?

Home is the safest place on earth, or should be. Was Ellie mad to leave it? I don't think so. A home is only a home because you belong there. Otherwise it's just bricks and mortar, just a house (or a caravan if you're a traveller, or an igloo if you're an Inuit). Ellie had just seen her baby self snatched by a stranger, and now her own mother and father and little brother could neither see nor hear her.

I'm nobody.

I don't belong anywhere.

I'm nobody.

I don't belong anywhere.

That was all she did think, once she was out there, because the wind didn't give her chance to think. It pushed and pulled her, and if she opened her mouth it rushed in, and she swallowed it in great cold gulps. She waded through it, along the little cul de sac where she lived, right at the Green Man and into the High Street. As she turned the corner the wind came funnelling down with a force that nearly knocked her off her feet.

By now the street was almost deserted. Cars went by with their headlights on and leaves danced in the beams like snowflakes. Ellie put her head down and started to battle her way towards the town centre, and the library. You can guess why she was going there. She was going to unbreak a promise.

Let him be there let him be there let him be there!

I should never have tricked him.

It's all my fault.

I'll *give* him my bike, I will.

I'll have to pretend I lost it and Mum and Dad'll kill me.

Oh let him be there let him be there let him be there.

What if he *isn't*?

What if what if what if

What if I stay invisible *forever*?

She had her head down and couldn't see where she was going. Sooner or later she was bound to run into something – or someone.

Bang!

'Oops! Sorry!'

She looked up, and had to look a very long way because the man was so tall. He was wearing a long raincoat, and a hat pulled down over his eyes.

'You seen this boy?'

There were two men, one on either side, two pairs of hard eyes. A leather wallet was held out, and in it was a photograph.

'There's a reward.'

She stared at the spiky hair and curiously round eyes.

'It's him!'

The words were out before she could stop them.

'*What*?' Now a hand was on her shoulder. 'You've seen him! Where? When?'

'Today! Here – there – oh, where *is* he?'

'You'd better think hard!' the first man said. '*Where*?'

Now she looked at him properly for the first time, and didn't like what she saw. She didn't like the pale, narrow face, the thin lips, the slitted eyes. Whoever he was, this man was no angel.

She twitched her shoulder free and ran, but they came after her with long strides. One of them had her by the shoulder again.

'*Where*?'

Ellie thought fast.

'By the castle!' she gasped. 'He was – eating an ice cream, and – oh!'

Her shoulder was released so suddenly that she almost fell, but the wind caught and held her. She saw the first man beckon furiously and the other came and pushed right past her. They were going back the way they had come. They went with curious, thrusting strides, as if they were ice-skating. They went as if the wind was behind them, not against them.

They would be back soon enough, Ellie thought. The boy without a belly button would not be there. Why should he be? By now he was probably out of town.

He'll have gone back to wherever he came from.
I broke a promise.
And now I've told a lie.
Those terrible men will come looking for me.
Help!
They – *saw me*!
Mum didn't see me, or Dad or Sam.
They saw me!
Suck suck suck suck suck suck suck suck

The rag doll was lying on her bed at home. Ellie Horner was sucking her thumb again.

Six

ON THE RUN

Ellie did not know how long she crouched in the shop doorway sucking her thumb. Time seemed to have blown away with the wind. She was there because she didn't know what to do. She couldn't go forward and she couldn't go back. It felt as if she would have to stop there forever. Or until those two men came looking for her.

She shut her eyes to make the world go away. The trouble was, she could still hear it and feel it.

When she felt the tap on her shoulder she screamed. The hand that had tapped her started to shake her, but still she screamed.

'It's me! It's me!'

She heard the voice and knew it, even though she had only ever heard it once before. She opened her eyes and saw those other eyes, greeny-blue and round.

'Come on!' He held out his hand and she took it.

She never held hands with boys. Or rather, the only time she ever held hands with boys was when Miss Cole made the whole class stand in a ring for silly games. But she clutched that hand as someone falling from the top of a cliff clutches at the last tussock of grass to save herself.

She found herself holding the boy's hand and she found her legs working as she hurried to keep up with him. She was swallowing the wind in bucketfuls, and her eyes watered so that the street was wavy and blurred.

'Whoops! Look out!'

Now she was being dragged sideways. Then her cheek pressed against something rough and hard.

'What on earth—?'

'Sssh!'

He crouched beside her, coiled and ready to run. Above her were madly dancing leaves. They were under the oak that had not been there yesterday.

Then she saw them pass, hats pulled low over their eyes. Two tall men in long raincoats, striding, gliding. They looked to left and right but they did not see the pair behind the brand new oak. On they went, carving the wind.

'Gone!'

'But – they went the other way! They went to the castle!'

'They're everywhere,' he said.

'You mean – they can be in two places at *once*?'

She was going to have to believe him if he said so.

'I mean the place is crawling with them.'

She looked sideways at him. He was as white as she felt.

'They're looking for you,' she told him.

'I know.'

'I told them I'd seen you by the castle.'

'Thanks.'

'But why? Why are they looking for you?'

'Oh, mind your business, Ellie Horner!'

It took a moment for it to sink in.

'How—? You know my name!'

'Course!' He sounded scornful, as if she should have known that as a matter of course.

'So what's yours?'

'Told you – I'm an angel.'

'They have names – course they do! Gabriel and such!'

He shrugged. He was not looking at her or even listening properly. His eyes were flicking beyond her, left and right.

'Well, I'll have to call you something. I'm not calling you angel, if that's what you think!'

'Suit yourself.'

'I will. I'll think of a name, then call you it.'

There was no reply. The wind blew, the leaves shook and rattled. The world was still dark. In the wild darkness she named the angel.

'Plum!'

She hoped it would annoy him. It was not particularly angel-like. But then, nor was the boy.

'D'you like it? Plum!'

'Let's go!'

He was off and she went after him. She didn't have much choice. For all she knew he was the only one in the whole world who could see her. He, and the tall men. He was going back the way she had come, back towards the end of town and her own house.

'Where are you going?' she screamed, but he kept on.

Ahead was the Green Man, the filling station lit like a Christmas tree, and beyond them the spire of the church. Its clocks counted her days aloud. It divided them into hours and quarters, and had from the beginning. As a baby she had lain and listened to its chimes, and now she had them in her bones. That, and the roar of trains.

When he turned into the cul de sac she knew where he was going.

'No! No! You can't go there!'

What did he mean to do? Knock on the door? Say to her mother 'Oh hi, I'm an angel. Don't believe me? Like a tree in the garden, would you? Got a plum stone handy?'

'No! No!' She grabbed at his arm.

He tugged it free and ran ahead. He ran straight up the drive of her own house, under the carport and round the back.

She saw that the curtains of the living-room were still undrawn. The window made a glowing rectangle of light. Slowly she went towards it and looked in. There sat her father, Sam by his chair still playing with his farmyard. Beyond them she saw her mother, laying the table with the blue-and-white plates.

I'm like the little match girl, she thought. She was gazing in at a world she could not share. That story always made her cry, and now the scene went blurred.

She squeezed her eyes tight shut. Fiercely she willed time to go backwards. She wanted time to go back to this morning, to the moment when she had started spitting plum stones outside the library.

You know the feeling. It's called 'if only'. There are people everywhere, all the time, playing the 'if only' game. People in hospital with broken legs, thinking 'If only I hadn't rushed out this morning without brushing my teeth, I wouldn't have been in the road at the exact same moment as that car.' Burglars in prison thinking 'If only I'd remembered my torch, I wouldn't have tripped over that wire and fallen and woken the whole house up.' I expect you've done it yourself.

If only I'd never bought those plums.

And even if I had, if only I'd gone straight home.

If only I hadn't even spoken to that
boy.

But she had. And as far as we know, time can't
go backwards. Certainly not for the wishing. It can
stand still, of course, but we'll come to that later.

It's been dark for ages, but soon it'll be
properly dark.

Then what?

I hate the dark. I hate it, I hate it.

She turned from the window and looked round
for the boy. She needed him, because he could see
and hear her. Without him she was a ghost.

He had found her bike, the one she had promised
him. He looked at it and then he looked at her. She
knew what he wanted her to do.

It was the stupidest thing she had ever done, to
bet him that bike against a pair of wings. But how
was she to know? She had lost the bet and broken
the promise, and felt in her bones that she was to
blame for the wind and the darkness and the way
the world had changed.

Even now she tried to change the subject.

'We could sleep under here, I suppose.'

She pointed. Along one side of the garden were

54

three stone arches, under a humpbacked footpath that led across the railway line. A single track ran along a deep cutting at the end of the garden, behind a high wooden fence. From time to time a train roared by, familiar and unnoticed as the ticking of a clock. Only at night would Ellie sometimes hear them as she lay awake in the darkness, and wonder dreamily where they had come from and where they were going.

'Look – there's plenty of room.'

She led the way. The first arch was the lowest, the third the highest. They all went right back into a darkness where she could hardly make out the lawn mower, the garden chairs, the barbecue. The wind was rattling the leaves at their feet and Ellie gave a little shiver.

She remembered that she had something to tell, a thing more awful even than the tall striding men in raincoats.

And so she told him. She told him the old story, the one she had known all her life, and loved, because it was about herself, and had a happy ending. She told what she had seen barely an hour ago.

'But it went wrong,' she ended, and she was

half-sobbing with the terror of it. '*The dog never came!*'

There was a little silence that was not a real silence because of the moaning of the wind and creaking of the high trees.

'I know,' he said at last, slowly, grudgingly almost.

'You *what*?'

'I'm not just any angel.' Another wind-filled silence. 'I'm your guardian angel.'

SEVEN

FLYING

It was ages before Ellie could take it all in. They
squatted on upturned boxes in the first arch, and
talked the whole thing through. Plum (we must
call him that, because Ellie does, but I think it
more likely that his name was Raphael or Gabriel)
was the large dog that had frightened the thieving
stranger from the garden all those years ago.

'You can turn yourself into a *dog*? Go on then
– do it!'

You can hardly blame her. You or I would have
said exactly the same.

'I could,' he said. 'Can't now.'

'Oh, *that's* handy! I can turn myself into a bear.
A parrot. A kangaroo. Least – I could once.
Can't now.'

'I was guarding you,' he said.

'Well, pity you weren't this afternoon!'

'I know,' he agreed miserably. 'I'm sorry.'

She stared at him, and the full meaning of what he was saying began to sink in.

'You mean you've been there my whole life?'

'Yes.'

'The *whole time*?'

'Yes.'

It was spooky. She didn't like it. Her life was private.

'What – even when I was at school? On holiday?'

'Yes.'

'Even – even when I went to the lav?'

'Yes. Everywhere. All the time.'

She didn't believe him. None of us believes what we don't want to, and neither you nor I would like to believe we were being watched the whole time. Watched when we pinch stuff from the fridge, watched when we tell fibs, watched when we pick our noses or write rude words on the wall.

'Prove it.' she said.

'How?'

'Right. What – what did I have for Christmas last year?'

'That bike,' he replied promptly.

'Anyone could've guessed that. What else?'

'Monopoly, felt tips, pencil case, matching red hat and scarf, a watch that—'

'Stop!'

She looked at him, fair and skinny and pop-eyed, and was all at once shy. This boy really was an angel. Wings or no wings. The trouble was, he didn't look like one, let alone act like one. If ever she had needed an angel it was now. And if a proper one had come flapping down, with great snowy wings and praying hands and edged with gold . . .

'I wish you looked more like an angel,' she told him.

'Sorry.'

'Show us your belly button again.'

He obliged without a word. She stared at the pale, perfectly smooth skin.

Two and two make four.

You can't make it five, even if you try.

And you *do* need a belly button to be born.

You might as well admit it.

He is an angel.

Wings or no wings.

She drew a deep breath.

'OK. I admit it. You're an angel.'

'Thanks.'

'And – I broke my promise. The bet. Here – take it.'

The bike was propped against the stone wall of the arch. He looked at it and brightened.

'You sure?'

'Sure.'

She took the handlebar and gave it a little push towards him. It was probably the hardest thing she had ever done. She had begged and begged for that bike ages before her parents gave in. She had even prayed for it. If she lost it, they'd never buy her another. Never. It felt as if she were giving part of herself away.

She looked up, her eyes brimming, and saw that Plum was watching her and that he seemed to be shining, as if the sun had suddenly come out. He stood lit in the windy darkness, and was smiling. She blinked, and by the time the tears had spilt and she could see properly again, he was just the same as ever.

'Thanks,' he said.

'It's what you came for, isn't it?'

He shook his head.

'Couldn't have taken it. You had to give it. And oh wow, you've done it, and – here, let's try!'

He swung his leg and sat on the saddle and grinned, and she could have killed him.

'Go!' he commanded.

'Don't you know about bikes? They don't *go*, you have to—'

But he was already pedalling furiously up the path.

'Go go go! Wheeeeee!'

The bike took off. It lifted like a plane, front wheel tilted, and flew steeply up to miss the tall tree that bordered the railway. Plum was still pedalling hard and now the bike was reared almost upright, and still it looked as if it might crash into the high branches. Ellie gasped and shut her eyes.

Afterwards she wished she hadn't, because she missed the moment when Plum cleared the tree and was properly airborne, above the trees, the houses, the telegraph poles. By then she could hardly make him out in the darkness, though she heard his voice blown faintly on the wind.

'Look at me! Look at meeeee!'

'Come back!' she screamed. 'Come back!'

She strained into the inky sky. Now he was showing off, doing loop the loops and tight, spiralling circles. He looked like their paper-boy – a mad paper-boy in the sky.

He's forgotten me.

He's got what he wanted and now he's going.

Doesn't need wings, now he's got my bike.

Goodbye, Plum.

Mean thing.

He's going to leave me like this.

She felt her aloneness and shivered. She looked fearfully about and saw the yawning caves beneath the arches. Leaves rustled and scuttered about her feet and she could smell them, and the cold stone and the earth.

This is where I belong now, out here.

P'raps it's where I'll have to live my whole life.

I'll be like an invisible bag lady, wandering the world.

I'll find my food in bins.

I'll sleep under hedges and in shop doorways.

I don't believe it!

I can't, I can't!

She ran across the lawn and reached the back door and hammered on it with her fists.

'Let me in!' she sobbed. 'Let me in! It's me, Ellie!'

Whether her voice was blown away by the wind she did not know. Perhaps that and the beating fists were drowned by the sound of the television. Or worst of all, what she feared was still true. That her own mother and father, her own brother, could neither see her nor hear her.

She turned away. She did not even try the handle of the door. Nothing, nothing could be worse than to be an invisible, silent stranger in your own home. At least out here she was real. The wind blew her hair and filled her mouth with its clean coldness as if she existed like anybody else.

Plum landed. She could hardly believe it. There

he was, sudden as ever in his entrances, at her elbow when she least expected it.

'There you are! Thought you weren't coming back!'

'What? No chance.'

Of course. That was his job. Always to be at her elbow, visible or invisible.

'I know where you are,' he told her.

'What?'

Of course he knew. She was right under his nose.

'Not that far away,' he said. 'Thing is – how'll we do it?'

'Do what?'

'Rescue you.'

Then she saw what he was talking about. Again she shivered. The baby she once was had been stolen by a stranger. That must have been the moment when her ten-year-old self had disappeared. Now she *was* that baby.

'I'm not real any more,' she said bleakly.

'You won't be, if we don't get that baby back.'

'Where is it, then? You saw it! Where? How?'

'X-ray eyes,' Plum told her.

'*What*?'

'See through things. You're – it's – in a house, and so is she.'

'That woman?'

'Forest Road. Number thirteen Forest Road.'

'She's – she's not going to *kill* it – me?' Her voice came out as a whisper. She stared into his silvery eyes and the cold air flowed between them.

'Not exactly,' he said at last.

'What do you mean?'

'She wants – she wants to take you – *there*.'

Now it was his turn to shiver. He wrapped his arms about his thin body.

'Where?'

'The Land of the Starless Night.'

He flinched as he spoke the words, as if they hurt. They struck Ellie to the heart.

'Oh no oh no oh no!' She repeated the words as if they were a kind of charm, to stop the terrible thoughts that were racing in her head.

Starless Night

Dark dark dark

I'll never be me again, ever.

If only if only if only.

I'm going to disappear into the dark.

I can feel myself going.

Suck suck suck

Suck suck suck

Suck suck suck suck

It seemed an age before she heard Plum's voice again. Even then, it seemed to come from a long way off.

'Stop it! Stop it!'

Then she was being shaken by the arm.

'You can't give up! You don't give in! Never!'

The words were stern and fierce. They sounded as if they were being said by a grown-up. She blinked the wind and the darkness from her eyes and saw him with that same pale glow she had glimpsed earlier. He had a kind of shining.

'They're after you and they're after me!'

'They? Those men?'

'And they've all been sent by *him*.'

'Who?' she screamed. 'I don't understand! Who?'

'Him.' He paused. 'They call him – the Boss.'

EIGHT

THE BOSS

'They're looking for you now, as well,' Plum told Ellie.

'How d'you know?'

'Because time hasn't turned backward.'

'What?'

'To the moment when you were stolen – nearly stolen.'

Ellie went dizzy at the thought.

'Don't you see? If you had been stolen when you were a baby, if I hadn't been there, the whole world would've been different. The whole story would be wrong. It would have to be wound back and played again.'

'Without me in it?'

It is hard to suck your thumb and put your hands over your ears at the same time. Ellie tried it. It isn't easy to think when you are terrified, either. She tried to work out what Plum was saying.

It was like the butterfly's wing. If just one butterfly flapped its wings in a steamy rainforest thousands of miles away, the whole world changed. She had heard that ages ago, but was not sure whether she believed it. If it was true, then it meant that even a baby being there or not could change the world. There would be tiny shifts and changes, but they would spread out and change other things, and then *those* things would change, and—

She gave up. She tried to stop thinking altogether. That isn't easy, either. Sometimes, when people were saying things she didn't want to hear, she said rhubarb rhubarb rhubarb over and over again inside her head. Sometimes it worked. She tried it now.

Rhubarb rhubarb rhubarb
Why is this happening to me?
Rhubarb rhubarb rhubarb
I wish time would go back, and I'd go back
to when I bet him the bike and I'd *give* him
the pesky thing and then perhaps none of
this would ever have happened and—

Rhubarb rhubarb rhubarb

Why did that—

Rhubarb rhubarb rhubarb rhubarb

'Why did that woman steal me?'

She said the last words out loud without realising.

'For him, of course,' Plum told her. 'The Boss.'

'But why me?'

'Oh, you're nothing special. He tries to get everyone, all the time. He's got a list – and everyone's on it. You just happened to be next, that's all.'

Ellie didn't know whether to be glad or sorry. She had rather thought herself something special. We all do. And we're right, in a way. You're special because there's only one of you. There's no one else exactly like you in the whole world. Even if there's someone who looks like you, they could still have a different number of eyelashes, or a mole on their back, or something. And they'd still be different inside, invisibly. They'd have different thoughts and feelings. And it's thoughts and feelings, not just the way you look, that make you who you are. And now it looks as if we're on the Boss's list, so we'd better all look out.

'We've got to get that baby back this minute!'

'I know,' Plum said. 'We'll try the easy way first.'

'What? Knock on the door and ask?'

'Something like that.'

'What?'

She had hated the look of that tall dark woman, and liked the sound of the Boss even less.

'I knock at the front door. You nip in at the back and grab the baby.'

'Oh *yes*! And what if she grabs me?'

'And we'll take the bike. That way, at least one of us can escape.'

'Oh yes! You again!'

'Sometimes,' Plum said, 'I get really fed up of being an angel.'

'Good,' Ellie said. 'Because it doesn't look as if you'll be one much longer. Are we going, or what?'

She wanted to get it over, the whole thing. Whatever was going to happen, she wanted it to happen soon.

Plum said he would ride the bike. The men in raincoats were looking for an angel, and angels don't ride bikes. He said rather proudly that he was probably the only angel in the history of the world to ride one.

'Oh, that'll be really really nice!' Ellie said. 'So they just grab me!'

'No, they don't. They don't know it is you. They don't know, because you don't *look* like you. Fair hair or dark? Blue eyes or brown?'

'What?'

He was telling her that he would just wave a wand or something and change the way she looked. She was amazed by how affronted, how absolutely furious she felt at the suggestion. She'd looked in the mirror enough times and wished she did look different – we probably all have. As a matter of fact, she did rather regret her hair, which was wild and curly and wouldn't hang straight and silky the way she wanted it. She also thought her nose could be just the teeniest bit shorter, though more on some days than others. Some days her face seemed to be all nose.

Now, however, the very idea of being changed in the twinkling of an eye made her mad.

'Don't you dare!' she spat.

'Keep your hair on. You'll be safer, that's all. Go on – go ginger with a million freckles!'

'You do and I'll – I'll—.' She was stuck for a threat that might warn off an angel. She would have liked to threaten to smash his harp, or at least snap its strings. 'Change yourself!'

'Can't. I told you. Can't do anything for myself.'

'Some angel. Tough. Well, you're not doing it to me!'

She already felt that she only half-existed. If she looked different, she would have vanished completely.

There'd be a hole in the world.

An Ellie-shaped hole.

Even Mum and Dad wouldn't know me.

Or Sam.

Rhubarb rhubarb rhubarb rhubarb

Oh, but there's *already* an Ellie-shaped hole in the world!

And the Boss has got me – or halfway
got me.
The Land of the Starless Night . . .
Rhubarb rhubarb rhubarb
Dark dark dark.
Dark and nothingness.
I think I can feel myself going already.
Suck suck suck suck
Suck suck suck suck suck

'Have it your own way,' Plum said. 'Don't blame
me if you get nobbled. And if you keep sucking
your thumb like that it'll drop off. Come on.'

He started to push the bike. Ellie followed him.
She didn't have any choice. She had to force her
feet to move, drag them.

The town was almost deserted. It was tea-time
on Saturday and nearly everyone had gone home.
The eerie dark and the wind had driven them
away. They could not know that the Boss was in
town, but they hurried home to light and safety.
All, that is, but the tall men with hats pulled down
over their eyes, going in pairs, hunting.

The Boss kept in touch by radio. They reported
back.

'No sign at the castle. Over.'

'Park's all clear. Over.'

'Calling all units. Another drag of the main street. He's got to be here. He isn't going anywhere. He can't fly. My guess is that he and the girl are together. Even if they aren't – get one, and we've got 'em both. Repeat. All units to High Street.'

The Boss flicked off his control switch. In a dark corner of the room a baby started to cry. He got up and went and stood over it.

The face the baby saw above it in the dimness was not familiar. It did not know the dead eyes under the black bushy brows, or the twisting red lips in a narrow white face. It shut its eyes tight and tears squeezed out as it redoubled its cries.

'Shut it up!'

'Yes, Boss.'

The wolf-woman got up and went over swiftly. An icy draught went with her. She and the Boss had haloes of frost, their own private weather of a black and withering iciness. The baby was probably crying because it was cold, colder than any baby is meant to be.

The curtains of number Thirteen Forest Road

were closed against the darkness and the wind outside. There was no sound. It was as cold and silent as a tomb. It was the waiting room for the Land of the Starless Night.

NINE

TRAPPED

The town was crawling with men in raincoats. Ellie and Plum hurried from cover to cover. They dodged behind walls or into side streets. The wind was emptying the town and shops were beginning to close early. Doors were being banged shut and bolted, lights were going out.

In the end they were bound to be caught. They reached a side road just as two of the men were retracking to the High Street on the Boss's orders. They almost collided. Ellie shrieked.

'That's them!'

'Get 'em!'

'Lift off! Plum spun his wheels and tilted the bike skyward.

'Him – that's him!'

'Get her!'

Ellie looked wildly about then dived back and into the nearest shop. Mr Moon the butcher was

76

clearing his window, packing up for the day. He couldn't see Ellie, but looked up as the two men entered.

'Afternoon, gentlemen!'

'The girl – we're after the girl!'

'I beg yours?'

'She's in here somewhere!'

'Girl? What girl?'

'Where is she?'

'Not here. What about round the back?'

Ellie listened, crouching behind a chopping table, her nostrils filled with the beastly reek of raw meat.

'Here!'

Mr Moon sidestepped and blocked the way as the pair made for the back of the shop. He was built like an ox.

'Out! Or I call the police!'

One of the men shrugged.

'We'll wait outside. She'll have to come out.'

Mr Moon followed them to the door. Ellie heard him shut and lock the door.

'Girl?' he repeated. 'What girl?'

Ellie got up. Her legs were shaking and she felt cold. Even her brain seemed frozen.

Plum had got away on the bike, must have, or both the men wouldn't have come after her. Now they were waiting, would wait forever for her to come out. Perhaps there was a back way, and if she was quick enough she would find it before they did.

There was a door at the back. She went through and found herself in a small paved yard with high brick walls. On top of the walls were loops of barbed wire.

The two men couldn't get in here, but neither could she get out. Unless, of course, she had wings.

He got away all right.

On my bike.

I daren't go out the front way, they're waiting for me.

I'll have to stop here forever.

Rhubarb rhubarb rhubarb

I'll be locked in here all night.

In that horrible room with all that smelly meat.

If I was a sheep, and someone killed me to eat, I'd come back and haunt them.

Or a cow or a chicken or a pig.

How do I know their ghosts don't come out at night?

Ghostly sheep and cows and chickens and pigs, all bleating and mooing and squawking and snuffling.

And I've eaten them, I've eaten them all!

And they'll come after me, because I've eaten their relations.

I've had them with mint sauce and tomato ketchup.

Oh help please help help

Suck suck suck

Suck suck suck suck suck suck

She could see that awful jostling crew, all transparent with ribs and bones showing through. She began to think she preferred the Land of the Starless Night.

'Ellie! Ellie!'

At first she did not hear. Nor did she see Plum, whizzing above her round and round in circles, doing his mad paper-boy act. She had shut her eyes in the hope of making everything go away. It's a perfectly natural thing to do. I've done it. So have you. It has never worked, and it didn't now.

When Ellie opened her eyes she was still in that dismal little yard with the wind yanking her hair and making the panes of the windows rattle.

'Ellie!'

She looked up and saw him, a darker shape against the dark sky.

'Get – me – out!' she screamed, as if the pack of ghostly animals were already at her heels.

'Can't! How can I?'

'You *must*!' She stamped her foot, hard. It hurt.

'Told you. Can't.'

'So what shall I *do*?' She was dizzy from craning up into the dimness.

'The butcher! Try the butcher!'

'What?' Ellie did not believe what she was hearing. '*What*?'

'Worth a try.'

CRACK!

CRACK CRACK!

'Got to gooooo!' The last word was on a long, rising note. The bicycle banked steeply and went spiralling up, and little orange flashes punctuated the darkness.

Guns! They've got guns!

They'll shoot him down – then what?

Rhubarb rhubarb rhubarb

I'll be alone . . . all alone . . .

Oh, poor Plum . . .

And what about my bike?

It'll drop down out of the sky and be smashed to smithereens.

Oh, what'll I tell Mum and Dad?

Oh, I haven't got a mum and dad!

And soon I won't have a guardian angel, either.

Not that I'll need one, where I'll end up.

Rhubarb rhubarb rhubarb rhubarb

Oh, if only I'd never bought that bag of plums!

There she goes again. Playing the 'if only' game. Mind you, you can't blame her. There she is, trapped in the tiny back yard of the butcher's shop. Its walls are high and topped with barbed wire. Out front are two men – probably more, by now – with guns. She's between the devil and the deep blue sea. She's on the horns of a dilemma. She's between a rock and a hard place. And that's before you even think about the ghostly animals that might haunt the shop.

Plum disappeared. The gunshots stopped. Ellie could hear Mr Moon inside the shop, still tidying up. Plum had said to try the butcher. What had he meant? At the moment she had only two choices – stay or go. Wait for Mr Moon to unlock the front door and rush out with him into the dangerous street. Did she really have a third choice?

She began to remember what a nice man Mr Moon was. How he whistled as he chopped and sliced. How he always joked with her mother, and had come right out of the shop to look at Sam when he was a new baby in his pram. And how once he had admired him, he had winked at Ellie and slipped her a toffee.

Mr Moon appeared at the back door with a pile of boxes. He came out and dumped them in a corner. Then he would go back in and lock up. It was her last chance. Ellie dived back in through the open door, and was again in the room where whole red carcases hung on hooks in huge freezers, and big knives and choppers lay on wooden blocks. She went through to the shop, now very empty, with its gleaming enamel trays edged with bright green plastic parsley.

'Oh!' She let out a little shriek.

There outside were the two men, hats pulled down, collars up, waiting. She ran back before they could see her. Mr Moon was pushing home heavy iron bolts, and whistling.

It was probably the whistling that decided her. If people whistle, at least it means they're human.

'Mr Moon!'

He turned, and stopped whistling as he cast an eye round for any last jobs he might have missed.

'Mr Moon!'

He frowned. He frowned, then shook his head. He began to untie the strings of his blue-and-white striped apron with his thick, reddened fingers.

'Mr Moon – can you hear me?'

He stopped tugging at the string and seemed to listen.

'Can you? Oh please say yes or no!'

'Sounds like a kiddie,' Mr Moon muttered.

'Well, there ain't no kiddie here, and that's for certain positive.'

'Oh there is, there is!' Ellie was sobbing with relief. 'You can hear me. And I'm here, I'm really here!'

'First I thinks I hears gunshots. Now I'm hearing voices.'

'They *were* gunshots! I heard them too – and saw them!'

'You did?' He had not the least idea who he was talking to, but seemed to be having a conversation anyway.

'It's those awful men! The ones who chased me in here.'

'The girl? You're her?'

'Yes! I did run in here, it's just that you couldn't see me. Nobody can – not even my own mum and dad and it's all my fault and help me, please help me, Mr Moon!'

He sat down suddenly on a high stool. His face was a shade of greenish-white.

'You – know my name.' It came out as a croak. 'Time I took a holiday.'

'I know your name because my mum shops here – and me. I've often—'

'What's your name?'

'Ellie. Ellie Horner.'

She watched him anxiously. It was make or break time.

'Mrs Horner. Her with the little lad – and you're telling me—?'

'Yes! Yes, honestly.'

'So – what're you doing going round invisible?' he sounded disapproving, as if he thought she should know better.

'I – it'll take too long to tell. But I will tell you, I will, if you'll help me. Those two men are still out there waiting. And they've got guns.'

'Those cracks just now – guns?'

'Yes! Yes!'

He got up and went heavily to the half-open door leading to the shop. After a moment he turned.

'You're right. Still there.' He went over to a telephone that was fixed to the wall. 'Police, I reckon.'

He made the call.

'Two of them, with guns. Both wearing long coats, belted in, and hats. Yes – guns. And there's another witness.'

The call made, Mr Moon moved to the sink and noisily filled a kettle. He rinsed two mugs, one marked Bovril and the other Oxo.

'We'd best make tea,' he announced. 'And you know why?'

'Why?'

'Because,' he said, 'I wants to see that mug raised up and drunk from and put down empty, and then I'll know you're there invisible!'

'I don't blame you,' said Ellie miserably. 'You won't tell the police, will you?'

'Not an offence, as far as I know,' Mr Moon said. 'Nothing in Neighbourhood Watch about invisible.'

His eyes went to a pinned up tea towel picturing the Queen in full regalia.

'God Save the Queen,' he remarked. 'This is a funny old day, all right. All that dark and wind, and now girls gone invisible and men with guns. I shall wake up from this dream any minute.'

'I wish,' Ellie said. 'Nightmare, more like.'

She thought of Plum out there, cycling over the chimney pots, and wondered if he was frightening the birds.

CRACK!
CRACK! CRACK!
They both jumped.
'Plum!' screamed Ellie.

TEN

THE JIGSAW

They both made for the connecting door and peered round it. The plate-glass window was lit by wheeling blue light. From beyond came muffled shouts.

Mr Moon strode forwards and began pushing back bolts and turning keys. Ellie followed, but cautiously. The police wouldn't see her, but those men could. For all she knew, they could transmit death rays with their eyes at close range.

Mr Moon opened the door and the wind blew in.

There were two police cars. The men were already cuffed and being bundled into them. The policemen pushed down on the top of their heads, like they did in *The Bill*. An officer stood nearby talking on his radio.

'There *what*? *How* many? Yes. Yes. On our way.'

He saw Mr Moon.

'Mr Moon? You reported this?'

'Neighbourhood Watch. Area Organiser. Who are they? What's their game?'

He was peering into the car to see for himself what kind of men pursued small girls and started shooting in the High Street.

'We'll need a statement later.'

'What's going on?'

'We're taking these back to the station, then going out again. More sightings. We've already picked up four by the castle.'

Ellie saw what had happened. A call had gone out for two men in long belted coats, and wearing hats. And they were all over town. They stuck out a mile in the emptying streets. The police must think it was Christmas.

She longed to tell them that the Boss was in town, and a baby had been stolen. But she would not know how to begin to explain, even if she had been visible.

'Thank you, sir. We'll be in touch.'

The cars sped off.

'Good bit of excitement, that,' Mr Moon remarked. 'I'm a fan of *The Bill*, myself.'

'Me too,' Ellie said. 'Thank you, Mr Moon – you saved my life.'

'Could be,' he agreed. 'And you invisible, and all. Might I ask – are you intending to come visible? Soon?'

'Not up to me. I didn't choose it, you know.'

'People don't go invisible, of course,' he said, more or less to himself. 'Not to my knowledge.'

'Or mine,' Ellie said. 'Except in fairy tales or something.'

'So are you going to tell me what happened?'

Mr Moon made the tea and poured it steaming into the Bovril and Oxo mugs. He scooped his newspaper from a battered armchair and sat down heavily. Ellie perched on the high stool by the chopping board, and began. Mr Moon was a good listener. He didn't interrupt, only shook his head from time to time, or whistled through his teeth or took deep gulps of his tea.

'So now do you see?' said Ellie, when she had finished.

'I hear what you say,' he said, 'but I still don't see. What's it all about? This angel – this Plum – he really is an angel?'

'I told you. He's got no belly button.'

'That certainly does seem a clincher,' he admitted. 'So – where's he now, d'you think? I should like to meet him, I certainly should.'

'I don't know. What if he got hit and fell out the sky, and he's lying hurt somewhere? No one'd know and be able to help him! No one can even see him, except me.'

'And them,' he reminded her.

'I must go and find him, I must!'

'I think you should go home,' Mr Moon told her.

'No! I can't! They can't see me! It's horrible!'

'Me neither. But we're having a regular conversation. You go home and tell your mum.'

'But they can't hear me, either!'

'Is that a fact? Rum, that. So why can I?'

'I – I don't know. In any case – what about the baby? We've got to rescue it.'

'Ah. The baby. I was forgetting that.'

'That baby's *me*!'

So it was. Plum hadn't forgotten that, either. It was as much his fault as Ellie's that the baby had been taken. More, in fact. Guardian angels are meant to look after people, not go making silly bets with them about plum stones and bicycles.

'If only I'd never made that bet!'

He wheeled moodily among the chimney pots, playing the 'if only' game. Plum had plenty of 'if onlys' to think about. If only he hadn't fooled around so much, he'd never have lost his wings. If only he had his wings he might be able to save that baby, even now.

Plum was as nifty as any paper-boy when it came to trick cycling. He'd easily dodged the bullets. He'd had a bird's eye view of the police operation in the town, and seen dozens of men in raincoats being bundled into police cars and driven off. And he saw straight through the roof and ceilings of Mr Moon's shop, to where the butcher and Ellie were drinking tea and talking.

He was her guardian angel, but he hadn't done much about saving her. She'd done that herself, by dodging back and running into the shop. Not many brownie points there. And brownie points were what he needed, if ever he was going to get his wings back and be a proper angel again.

As a matter of fact, he thought he might be able to feel his wings growing back already. In Ellie's garden, when she had given him the bike, he had felt a curious prickling of his shoulder blades. A warm feeling, as if he were bathed in sunlight, had spread right through him.

He took one hand from the bar and reached across the other shoulder and felt. Yes! Feathers! The bike swayed and tilted and he grabbed the handlebar to steady it again.

'Oh wow! They're coming back! Wings! Oh wow!'

He pedalled like mad and put the bike into a perfect loop the loop, riding the wind that swept the roofs and shook the television aerials. A small girl looked out of her window, because the wind was so strong that she thought perhaps she might actually see it. And because now and then you can see angels – just glimpses – she saw Plum. She didn't exactly see him, and certainly not his newly sprouting wings. But she did see a sort of shining wheel turning in the dark sky, and ran down to tell her mother she had seen a UFO.

Nobody in the town would have been surprised to see a UFO that night (and by now it was nearly night). The proper darkness had fallen. They did not know exactly what was going on – how could they? And of course, in a way it was nothing to do with them. But if you are caught up in a story, even someone else's, you have to play your part in it. The Boss and the wolf-woman and their gang had come to town to get Ellie and bag an angel. And if that meant a mighty wind and the town being nearly blown away – well, that's the way the cookie crumbled.

Then Plum broke a rule. It was breaking rules that had lost him his wings in the first place, and you'd think he had learned his lesson. One of the rules, if you're a guardian angel, is that you keep your target in sight. You know where he or she is at all times. Plum knew that Ellie was with Mr Moon, all right, but he didn't know what her next move might be. He should have hung around and found out.

Instead, he did another turn and headed for

Forest Road. He didn't exactly have a plan for rescuing the baby all by himself, but hoped that one would come to him out of the blue. Things do sometimes come out of the blue, of course, but you can't count on it. Even if you're an angel.

At Thirteen Forest Road the Boss was getting the jigsaw out. This was terrible news. It meant that he had his back to the wall and was dangerous, even more dangerous than ever. One by one the crackling radios of his men had gone silent. He knew what had happened. One of them had managed to croak 'Look out, Boss – the fuzz!' before his radio went dead.

'It's you and me now,' he told the wolf-woman.

The baby was sleeping now, and she was watching it with a kind of fierceness, as if she wanted to eat it.

'You, me – and the jigsaw.'

The Boss had the biggest jigsaw in the world. It didn't just have hundreds of pieces, or even thousands, it had billions, squillions. The jigsaw *was* the world, a picture of it dreamed up by the Boss himself. He used it to make things happen.

He didn't have the whole jigsaw with him. That was kept in his own territory, the Land of the Starless Night. He just had the section with Ellie's town on it. Everything was there – the High Street, the churches, the library and schools, Ellie's house and – number Thirteen Forest Road. (There *was* no number Thirteen, remember, not in the real world. But there was in the Boss's scheme of things.)

This jigsaw was jumbled up in large bags, but the Boss knew that there were two Ellie-shaped gaps in it. One was in Ellie's own house. The other was in Thirteen Forest Road. That second gap had appeared at the very moment the wolf-woman had snatched the baby from the pram in the garden. The minute that had happened, Ellie's fate was up for grabs.

The Boss had shaken the pieces out of the bags, and they lay scattered about him. The good news was that he had to fit all the pieces together to get his way. The bad news was that if he did, if he slotted that Ellie-shaped piece into the gap at Thirteen Forest Road before midnight, he had her! She was his, and would go forever into the Land of the Starless Night.

'You just keep that brat quiet,' he told the woman. 'We're running out of time. Start the clock.'

The wolf-woman nodded. She went over to the table where a clock stood. It looked as if it might be the first clock ever invented. All its works were showing – the wheels and levers and a brass pendulum. Her long hands were still mittened, and she clumsily turned a large key.

At once the clock sprang into life. The fingers rushed round the dial to show the exact time. Twenty-seven minutes past six. The pendulum began to swing and a loud ticking set up – tick tock tick tock – in the unnatural quiet of the room.

The Boss passed his hands over the scattered pieces in a queer, fumbling arc. He began to touch them, feeling their shapes with long white tapered fingers.

Oh. I forgot to mention. The Boss is blind.

ELEVEN

A LOST ANGEL

Back at Ellie's house, the Horners were growing restive. Mrs Horner certainly was. She grew tired of calling Ellie, and went up to find her.

The room, as we know, was empty. Mrs Horner turned on the light to make sure. A book was lying face down on the floor against the wall. The rag doll lay on the bed, which was rumpled, as if Ellie had been sitting on it.

'Funny,' Mrs Horner said. 'Could've sworn she was up here.'

She switched off the light and went downstairs. Mr Horner was still watching sport and Sam was playing with his farmyard.

'I never heard her go out,' Mrs Horner said.

'Door did open and shut, remember, a bit back,' Mr Horner reminded her, without taking his eyes from the screen.

'But she'd never go out without telling us.'

'Not usually,' he agreed.

'This *is* usually,' she snapped. 'And it's getting dark – properly dark.'

She opened the front door and the wind rushed in, lifting a newspaper from the floor and making the kitchen door slam.

'Such a wind!' She banged the door shut again.

'She'll be back for her tea,' Mr Horner told her.

'It's past tea-time now. She knows very well it is. I'm going to ring Alice's mother and see if she's there.'

Alice Foster was Ellie's best friend. They sat together at school and were the biggest gigglers in Miss Cole's class. They played together out of school, too. They made dens under the arches in the garden, and tracked people, and were always inventing things. For the past few weeks, though their mothers did not know this, they had been mixing things together to make an explosion. A really big bang. They mixed things from the kitchen, mostly. Flour and custard and vinegar and washing-up liquid and eggs and stuff. All they had managed to produce so far were evil-smelling brews, but they hadn't given up. Sooner or later, Ellie said, they'd hit the right combination, then – whoosh! The Big Bang.

Mrs Horner rang Mrs Foster. Ellie might be invisible but she had, as she herself realised, left an Ellie-shaped hole in the world. And her mother, for one, was going to make sure she filled it again.

When she found out that Ellie was not at Alice's house Mrs Horner rang several more people. None of them had even seen Ellie that day. Each time she put down the phone she felt a sense of dread. For some reason, a picture kept flashing into her mind of that long-ago day when a tall dark woman had appeared in the garden.

'I'm not giving it much longer,' she said. 'Then I'm ringing the police. And switch that thing off. I don't know how you can sit there watching when your own daughter's missing!'

'So now what, young lady?' Mr Moon asked. 'I've got a home to go to, and a missis.'

'And I've got to find Plum.'

'I'll tell you what,' he said. 'You walk along with me. I don't live far. You'll be safe with me.'

He didn't say it, but he thought there could still be gunmen out there. Ellie didn't say it, but so did she.

He locked up the shop, while Ellie stood shivering in the wind that seemed to have got colder with the fall of night. A cat blew by with its fur all anyhow and eyes screwed up in fury. Cats hate winds, even the ordinary kind. And all the cats in town knew this was no ordinary wind.

'You'd best hold my hand,' Mr Moon said.

A small warm hand slipped invisibly into his own great paw. He tried not to flinch, so as not to hurt her feelings. He had not come out this morning expecting to meet a ghost, or whatever you call people who are there, but invisible. He had certainly not dreamed of ending up holding hands with one.

They more or less had the streets to themselves, though they weren't exactly quiet and empty. Litter blew by, tin cans rattled, newspapers reared up like pale phantoms and here and there bowled a hat whose owner had given up chasing it.

There was no sign of Plum or the bicycle, though Mr Moon was almost as keen to find them as Ellie herself. He had gone all his life without so much as a glimpse of an angel, and was inclined not to believe in them. Now he was not so sure. So much had happened in the last hour that he thought he might now swallow even an angel called Plum, and riding a bicycle.

They peered over every wall into every garden, and explored every alley. Now and then Ellie called his name.

'Plum! Plum!'

But Plum had gone in the opposite direction and could not hear. By now he was right above Thirteen Forest Road and hovered there, as if he were treading water. He gazed down with his X-ray eyes, down through the roof, the attics and ceilings to the scene in the small front room.

They were still there, The Boss, the wolf-woman and the baby, but he knew that already. What was new, and what sent a shiver down his spine that had nothing to do with wings sprouting, was the jigsaw.

Plum knew about the jigsaw. He had been told

about it years ago, during his training. He knew that it was Bad News. Even top angels had referred to it in hushed voices. If the jigsaw was out, it was Count Down Time. He could not hear the heavy tick tock of the clock, but knew that it was relentlessly counting the seconds to go till midnight.

If the Boss could complete the jigsaw, and slot the Ellie-shaped piece into the Ellie-shaped gap in Forest Road, the game was over.

You might wonder why Plum did not go in now, and snatch the baby and whizz off with it on his bicycle. I'll tell you why. Because Thirteen Forest Road was the Boss's territory. You might say it was an extension of the Land of the Starless Night. No angel, not even the archangel Gabriel, could ever set foot there. It was ringed by an invisible barrier. Humans could go in there – the police could, if they knew about it. So could Ellie herself, if she dared. But not Plum.

He and Ellie would have to make the rescue together. He spun the bike round and headed back towards the butcher's shop.

By now Ellie and Mr Moon had reached his house, and needless to say had not found any fallen angel.

'Oh dear!' Ellie had to blink away a tear that she hadn't even realised was there.

'I'm sorry about that,' Mr Moon told her. 'I really am. We'll have to hope the poor little chap flew off in time, and didn't get hit.'

'But now I've lost him anyway! I'll never find him!'

'He'll find you,' Mr Moon told her. 'Not much of a guardian angel if he doesn't.'

'That's the whole point! He's not! I think that's why he lost his wings!'

Mr Moon was local representative for Neighbourhood Watch. He thought a good deal about crime. He did not think it wise for a small girl to be roaming the streets at night, even an invisible one. Particularly as he knew that the police were all engaged on other business. And, having saved Ellie's life, he now felt an extra interest in her. Besides, he liked her.

'I expect you're hungry?' he asked.

'What? Oh, yes. I am a bit.'

'I'll tell you what. You come in and have a bite to eat. Then—'

'Oh, but—'

'You can't find him. Let him find you. See down through the roofs of houses, you say?'

'Yes, but—'

'Then he can find you as easy inside as he can out.'

Put like that, the idea seemed reasonable.

'And Mrs Moon can give you a nice supper – and him as well, if he turns up.'

Ellie was tempted.

True, that is.

He *can* see through roofs.

Easier for him to find me than for me to find him.

But he won't know where Mr Moon lives!

Oh, and the police might not have caught all those men!

There could still be some out here, looking for me.

They could shoot me dead!

Oh dear oh dear oh rhubarb!

A small voice inside her head was telling her it wasn't a very good idea. But an even louder voice was telling her she might be shot dead. No prizes for guessing which one won.

'All right,' she said.

What the small voice was telling her was that if Plum was still alive he would be up in the air, and scouring the town for her. He would be able to see whole streets at a glance. But if Ellie went into Mr Moon's house it would be a different story. Plum would have to cycle over the roofs of every single house, looking down into them one after another. First one side of the road, then the other. First one street, then another.

Ellie knew all this at the back of her mind, but went in with Mr Moon anyway. You can't blame her. No one wants to get shot dead. And her guardian angel was supposed to be looking after her, not the other way round.

Ellie went into Mr Moon's house for supper. Plum was on his way back to the butcher's shop to find her. And at thirteen Forest Road the Boss was slotting in pieces of the jigsaw, the baby was sleeping, the wolf-woman nodding and the clock was ticking away the seconds to midnight.

TWELVE

STILL LOST

Ellie didn't know exactly what Mr Moon told his wife. They went into the kitchen and shut the door. She could hear their voices, but not what they were saying.

She looked round the living-room. Somebody, probably Mrs Moon, collected small china animals. There were rows of cats and dogs and foxes and lions and monkeys. She noticed there were no sheep or pigs or cows, and thought she knew why. No one, as far as she knew, went in for cat stew or monkey pie.

Someone, again probably Mrs Moon, was fond of stitching. The place was littered with embroidered mats and cushions. There was a tapestry portrait of the Queen above the fireplace. There were photographs, a lot of them showing Mr Moon with rod and line, and usually with a large fish. Pictures of him and his wife smiling outside a small caravan. Ellie found herself vaguely surprised that someone she knew only as the butcher actually had a home to go to, another life away from the shop.

The door to the kitchen opened.

'You poor little lamb!' exclaimed Mrs Moon.

It fleetingly occurred to Ellie that the real poor little lambs were stowed away as chops in Mr Moon's shop.

'Don't you worry about me not being able to see you,' Mrs Moon went on. 'Billy's told me all about it, and it's a crying shame, it really is. You really do wonder what the world's coming to.'

That was all right, then. Mrs Moon paused, then continued.

'Though I would take it kindly if you could just say a word. Just so's I know you are there. I mean, if Billy says you are, I'm sure you are. But if you could just say a word?'

'I'm here all right, Mrs Moon,' Ellie told her. 'I'm sorry to be a nuisance.'

'Oh my good gracious, it gives you quite a turn!' Mrs Moon sat down suddenly. 'Did it give *you* a turn, Billy, when you first heard it?'

'Not it, Kitty, *her*. And yes, I daresay it did come a bit surprising. But I'm used to it now, and so will you be in a bit. I told you. I know the little girl, she's in the shop regular.'

'Well, *that's* something!' said his wife, as if it made all the difference. 'And what's all this about angels being shot at?'

'Plum,' Ellie said. 'It's true. He was up in the air on my bicycle and they tried to shoot him down.'

'I never heard the like,' said Mrs Moon indignantly. 'Whatever kind of person goes round shooting at poor little angels?'

'I didn't get much of a look at them,' Mr Moon said.

'They could've shot you, Billy!'

'I suppose they could,' he agreed. 'Now, are you going to get us some supper, Kitty? This young lady's hungry.'

Mrs Moon went back into the kitchen. Mr Moon said, 'All we do now is sit tight till this angel of yours finds us. If he's lucky, he'll be in time for supper.'

★　　★　　★

Plum was aghast when he reached the butcher's shop, looked down and saw that both Ellie and the butcher had gone. Angels don't go in much for shopping, and it had never occurred to him that it was closing time. When the men shot at him for the second time he had biked off as fast as he could. After that, anything could have happened. He had to find out what – fast.

The first place Plum thought of looking was Ellie's own house and garden. She probably thought that was the safest place to be. He set off, pedalling against the wind.

His legs were beginning to ache and he would have given anything to have his wings back. He didn't use his legs much, as a rule, and certainly not to pedal a bicycle. The best part of being an angel was the flying, the great soaring arcs above the chimney pots, the dives and swoops. He loved being up there among the sparrows and pigeons and starlings, with the town spread out under him. He even liked it in the rain, and in the snow, flapping almost blind among the thick flakes. If ever he did get his wings back, he'd make very sure he never lost them again.

He battled his way against the wind till he saw ahead the lights of the Green Man and the filling station, and beyond that the steeple of the church. He began his descent. He went down, away from the sodium streetlights and into the darkness of the garden.

'Ellie?'

His eyes became accustomed to the dark and he could make out shapes of trees and bushes.

'Ellie!'

All he could hear was the wind and the moaning of high boughs and the scutter of leaves. He dropped the bike and went over to the high wall with its three arches. He felt a pang when he realised she could be huddled in there, cold and frightened.

But she wasn't. She was nowhere in the garden. A grumbling rumble started in the distance. It grew louder and louder and a train rushed by.

Plum mounted the bike and went up again until he was hovering right over the roof of the house.

Below, he saw Mr Horner watching the television. Sam, who had tired of his bricks, was looking at a book. He saw a table laid for tea, and Mrs

Horner fidgeting and glancing at the clock. She said something, and her husband got up from his chair, went to the front door and looked out.

He returned, shaking his head. Mrs Horner crossed the room, picked up the telephone and began to dial.

Ellie was not home. She was somewhere in the dark and windy town, and probably searching for him as desperately as he was searching for her.

The church clock began to chime the hour and Plum counted the strokes. Seven. Five hours to go.

At Thirteen Forest Road something curious was happening.

When first we saw the wolf-woman hurry in with the baby, she had opened the street door that led straight into a small front room. It was exactly the same as all the other front rooms on the street. Except of course that it had only the barest of furnishings.

There were certainly no china animals or lace mats or photographs. There wasn't even a carpet. (It is easier to make a jigsaw on bare boards.) Apart from the curtains, there were only a couple of chairs and, of course, the clock on its table. (The baby is lying in a kind of wooden basket, a trog.)

But now, several hours later, that small front room is becoming a big front room. It is growing. Already it is twice as big as you would think it could possibly be, judging by the outside of the house. It is growing with the jigsaw.

Every single part of the town is on the jigsaw. It has a castle, a park, schools, a library, a police station, four churches – I needn't go on. It's probably very like the town where you live. You won't ever have counted the number of shops, let alone the streets, roads, avenues and squares, and the number of houses. A jigsaw of it is not going to fit into your living room.

The Boss is blind, but his fingers are soft and clever and feely and have an instinct that guides them to the right places. That is not so impossible, if you think about it. Migrating birds find their way to Africa without a map or signposts. Swifts even do it in their sleep. A dog or cat will find its way home even from places it has never been, hundreds of miles away. Some people, particularly scientists, say they can explain everything. Don't believe it. The world is a deeply mysterious place.

Now the room where the Boss is working is already so big and empty that every sound is magnified. If you dropped a pin you would hear it. The baby has cried itself to sleep, and now and then a little shuddering sob runs around the walls. The pieces of the jigsaw go in swift and sure, click click. The tick of the clock could be that of Big Ben.

Tick tock tick tock tick tock.

The air in the room is getting colder, as if a frost is invisibly falling. The Boss does not feel it and nor does the wolf-woman. This is what they like, this is home. Cold and darkness.

THIRTEEN

A POLICE SEARCH

Plum was following a police car. He had seen
its blue light flashing below as he left Ellie's
house and headed back towards the town centre.
He did not have a clear plan in mind. He had stayed
ages back-pedalling over the roof of the house,
half-hoping Ellie might still turn up, wondering
what to do next if she didn't. Beyond the church
spire he saw the sky, faintly freckled with stars,
and wished he could be up there instead of here
in this messy world.

The police car was moving quite slowly. Plum
guessed that the hunt was still on for men going
in pairs, with guns. He was wrong, as he would
soon discover.

He cycled steadily just over and behind the
police car. He kept his eyes open in the hope of
spotting Ellie. They went past the library with its
new-grown oak, past the clock tower and towards

the castle. The car turned into a side street and Plum followed. Then he saw where they were going. The police station.

The two men jumped out and hurried in. Plum hastily propped the bike against a wall and followed.

'No joy, Jack,' they told the sergeant on the desk. 'Got a description? A photo?'

'Eleven years old. Skinny, with dark bushy hair. Wearing jeans and a yellow sweatshirt when last seen.'

'Any connection with the other business, d'you think?'

'Shouldn't have thought so.'

'How many did we get in the end?'

'Thirty-two.'

'Good grief! Those the guns – and radios?'

Plum saw the things piled on a desk.

'Any idea what's going on?'

'They won't talk. Not a dicky bird out of any of 'em. And I'll tell you another funny thing.'

'What?'

'No identification. No money. No keys. Nothing. Not even maker's labels in their gear.'

'You're joking.'

Plum saw his chance. He edged up to the desk and snatched up a radio. His heart thudded. No one could see him, so he couldn't be caught. But he'd never stolen anything before. He hoped that he wouldn't lose brownie points, and that stealing in a good cause would fall into the same category as a white lie.

He darted out, mounted the bicycle and took off again, heading for Forest Road. A plan began to take shape. He would talk to the Boss on the radio, pretending to be one of his men. He would tell him that one of the others had squealed, and the police were on their way to number Thirteen. Then, when the Boss and the wolf-woman rushed out, he would snatch the baby.

By the time he reached Forest Road Plum had seen all the holes in this plot, and knew that it wouldn't work. For one thing, he didn't sound anything like one of the Boss's men. He had tried it as he cycled over the castle shopping precinct.

'Boss – it's me, number eighteen!'

His voice came out as a croak, and set up a scare among the roosting pigeons above the supermarket.

They had spent the day riding the rollercoaster wind and needed to sleep. They peered frowstily above their tucked wings.

'Boss – warning! Red alert! The fuzz are on to us! Someone's squealed!'

It wouldn't fool anybody, let alone the Boss. The Boss hadn't got to be top man in the Land of the Starless Night by being taken in by stuff like that.

Plum nearly ditched the radio then and there. But perhaps he had a guardian angel, because he didn't. He hung on to it, in case it came in handy.

Now he was back to trying to find Ellie. He began to check out the streets of the town, one by one. Over the roof tops he went, a small windblown figure in a sky empty of birds.

Down through the roofs he looked, and saw people leading their own private Saturday night lives, without the least idea that they were being spied on. Why should they have? When people go into their house and shut the door and draw the curtains they think they are safe in their own cocoon, their own private world. That's what Ellie had thought, before she found out about Plum.

And of course the town was invisibly swarming with other guardian angels, because everybody has one. So where are they, you ask. Why don't they all come together to help Plum and beat the Boss and rescue that baby?

I'll tell you why. Because this is the story of Ellie and no one else. Every single person in that town has his or her own story – everyone in the world. You have. But you don't belong to Ellie's story, and nor do they. Only as far as they have to. They have all been blown about by the gale. Some of them have lost hats and tiles. And darkness had come early that particular September day. That's all.

It's different for Mr Moon, of course. He has been drawn into Ellie's story willy-nilly, and now so has his wife. They had never had children of their own and Mrs Moon, in particular, was sad about this. She had always longed for a little girl, one she could dress in frills and ribbons and embroidered pinnies. Now one had arrived in her house out of the blue, and in a funny kind of way made her wish come true.

It was a pity that she was invisible, but in some

ways that was even better. Mrs Moon pictured her dream child. She saw golden curls and round blue eyes, something like the pictures of Little Bo Peep and Mary Mary from the nursery rhyme books of her own childhood. The real Ellie was tall for her age and dark and skinny, with flyaway hair, and would not have been caught dead in the outfits Mrs Moon was imagining for her.

Ellie was tired of being invisible. She remembered that when she was younger she had thought what fun it would be. She could listen in to what people were saying, pinch burgers from McDonald's and go into films for the over-fifteens. She had rather supposed that being invisible made you into a sort of ghost, so that you could walk right through walls. It didn't. So if she went to Thirteen Forest Road she would have to go in through the door, like anyone else.

And she would have to do it soon. Ellie did not know about the jigsaw and the clock, but she could feel time breathing down her neck.

'I'll have to go now,' she said. 'Thank you for a lovely supper, Mrs Moon, but I've got to go.'

'What – in all this dark and wind and men shooting guns!'

'Yes. I've got to rescue that baby. Me.'

'This is the rummest thing I've ever heard,' Mr Moon said. 'I'll say that. Yes, I'll say that.'

'You stop here, Ellie, where you're safe,' Mrs Moon said.

'But I'm not safe! Don't you see? They've got the baby, and that baby's me!'

'Now hold on,' Mr Moon said. 'You know where this baby is, you say?'

'Thirteen Forest Road, Plum said.'

'Right. Missing Persons is the police's job. They'll go and get that baby out!'

'Of course!' A great flood of relief swept over her. The police had arrested the men with guns. Now they could arrest the Boss and the wolf-woman. She could hardly believe that the solution was so simple. (It wasn't.)

Mr Moon had some difficulty in making the policeman at the other end of the line understand. He wisely did not mention that the baby who had been kidnapped was actually Ellie Horner, and that she herself was now invisible and at his house. There is a limit to what you can expect the police to take in. He simply said that a baby had been snatched, and the gunmen arrested earlier were involved.

'It's at Thirteen Forest Road,' he told them.

'Whose baby is it, sir? There's a girl gone missing, but no reports of any baby.'

'Just go and get it,' Mr Moon said. 'We can sort all that out later.' He hoped.

'Name of Ellie Horner. Eleven years old and wearing jeans and a yellow sweatshirt. You haven't seen her, I suppose?'

'No,' replied Mr Moon with perfect truth. 'Sorry. And look, it was me that reported those gunmen earlier. Moon of Neighbourhood Watch. Now I'm telling you about the baby. I don't go in for wasting police time.'

'No, sir. Right. We'll look into it.'

Mr Moon put down the phone.

'That should do it,' he said. 'Everything'll be put to rights in no time. I take it you're wearing jeans and a yellow sweatshirt? They're looking for you, you know.'

'Yes! yes I am! Oh dear – poor Mum and Dad!'

'They'll be out of their minds!' cried Mrs Moon. 'I know I would be!'

'Not for much longer,' Mr Moon said. He looked in the direction Ellie's voice had come from and said, 'Once that baby's safe, you'll come visible again, I take it?'

'Oh yes! Yes! I hope so. Oh, surely I will? Oh, I wish Plum was here! He'd know.'

Plum, as we know, was scanning the rooftops of the town, one by one. It could be midnight before he found Ellie. That would be too late.

By then the Boss could have slotted the Ellie-shaped piece into the jigsaw. Then, at the very stroke of midnight, she would disappear. Forever this time – swallowed into the Land of the Starless Night.

FOURTEEN

THE SEARCH GOES ON

The Boss bent over the jigsaw and the right pieces seemed to fly to his fingers as if programmed. There was a soft click click as he slotted them in. By rights, it should take thousands of years for a blind man to complete that jigsaw. Steadily the town was taking shape. The castle was already there, two of the schools and rows and rows of houses. The walls of the room were still expanding, the air was growing colder by the minute.

The baby stirred and whimpered in its sleep. Suddenly the wolf-woman stiffened. Her head shot up, her nose twitched. A blue light was flashing in the street outside, It came in little bright stabs through the carelessly drawn curtains.

She rose in one swift movement and put an eye to the crack. There were three police cars, all with their blue lights wheeling and flashing.

Already people were coming out of their houses, hugging themselves in the cold, funnelling air.

The wolf-woman turned.

'The police, Boss.'

He carried on slotting in the pieces that seemed to glide to his fingers. Click. Click.

'They can't find us here.'

It was true. Already two bewildered policemen were checking the numbers of the houses.

'Doesn't seem to be a Thirteen!'

'You sure you got it right?'

'Do me a favour. Kidnapped baby, and someone gets the message wrong?'

'Who is it you're after?' The man from number Twelve came over in his shirtsleeves and eating a cheese and pickle sandwich.

'Haven't got a name. Number Thirteen.'

'You are joking!'

'What?'

'Hear that, Mick? Looking for number Thirteen! There ain't a number Thirteen. Never has been.'

His neighbour laughed and turned to tell his neighbour, and soon the message was passed right down the street.

The police held a hurried conference. One of them radioed back to base to check the address. The rest stood around feeling helpless and rather silly. The wind kept whipping off their hats, and they had to snatch at them or give undignified chase. They had come to raid an address that didn't exist. By now all the neighbours had come out and were talking and laughing. It was like an impromptu street party.

The officer in charge announced that they would search every house in the street.

'That'll wipe the smile off their faces.'

It did, too. No one wanted police ferreting round their houses on a Saturday night. Some of them, human nature being what it is, had things they didn't want the police to find. They hurried back in to hide them, but most were too late. The police may not have found a missing baby that night, but they did recover several items of stolen goods, including a laptop, silver candleabra, a bicycle and an oil painting of cows in a Scotch mist. The people who were caught did a lot of muttering about thirteen being unlucky for some.

Plum was several streets away while this sweep

was going on. He was buffeted by the wind and almost deafened by it. He thought he heard a kind of crackling. He steadied the bike with one hand and took out the radio.

'Calling all units, calling all units.'

The voice of the Boss struck terror into Plum. The bicycle rocked dangerously.

'Do not return to base. Repeat. Do not return to base.'

Plum held the radio at arm's length. This was the nearest he had ever come to the Boss. He knew only what he had heard from other angels. The Boss was evil, cunning and dangerous. Now his voice was being blown in splinters about the rooftops of the town. In that moment the Boss became more real, more close at hand than he had ever been. Plum could almost feel the frost of his breath.

He made no reply to the message. If he had tried, his voice would have come out as a mere squeak. He guessed that the Boss believed some of his men could still be out there, on the loose. It was even possible. Just because the police had pulled in thirty-two of them, it didn't mean that there had not been twice as many, three times.

He raised his eyes from the roofs and now saw blue fire licking into the sky from the direction of Forest Road.

'How on earth—?'

The Boss, the wolf-woman and the baby were in Forest Road. He knew that and Ellie knew that. Of course, one of the men in the cells could have squealed, but Plum doubted that. No one grassed up the Boss. No one dared.

Ellie must have told the police. He pictured her, knees knocking, in some telephone box making the 999 call. Ellie, alone now in the world and scared out of her life. Ellie, who he had known since the day she was born. He had been with her on her first day at school, splashed in the sea with her and turned somersaults of delight when she had at last been given the bike for Christmas. This bike. The one he was riding.

'I don't deserve to be her guardian angel.'

He had the unangelic thought that he wished he had taken one of the guns from the police station. Then he could have fired it through the window of the house in Forest Road and killed the Boss stone dead.

Even as he thought it, he knew that was impossible. No one could kill the Boss. All you could do was try to beat him at his own game. Even if you succeeded, he would be back. Plum could fire bullet after bullet at him, and he would still carry on slotting pieces into the jigsaw, while the clock ticked away the seconds to midnight and victory.

Plum knew that, and he knew too that the police would not be able to find number thirteen Forest Road. There was no such place, in the real world.

'I've got to find her! I must!'

He carried on, house after house, roof after roof, until his eyes began to ache and his head was spinning. He muttered under his breath 'Hang on, I'm coming! Hang on, I'm coming!'

Ellie was waiting patiently to hear the news that the baby was found and the nightmare over. The Moons were trying to behave as if this were just any ordinary Saturday night. Mr Moon was reading the sports pages of his newspaper, and his wife was embroidering a squirrel on a cushion cover. Both of them glanced up frequently. At any moment, Ellie could become visible, and they did not wish to miss that moment.

Ellie was turning the pages of a magazine Mrs Moon had given her. It was like being in the dentist's waiting-room. You turn the pages, but you aren't really reading.

I hope I get the all-clear.

Wish I hadn't eaten so much chocolate.

And fizzy drinks. They're bad as well.

What if I have to have one filled?

Or two? Or three?

Mum'll kill me.

Says I don't brush my teeth properly.

Like as if *she* knows what's going on in my mouth.

If I don't brush my teeth properly, she must have taught me wrong.

What if I have to have *ten* fillings?

Or a tooth out?

Or two or three or—

Debbie Parks knows how to make herself sick if she wants to get out of
something.

Wish I did.

Is it worse to be sick or have a tooth out?

And so on. That's all magazines in dentist's
waiting-rooms are for. That's why they're all
boring, and years old. No one even notices.

Ellie did try to read the magazine but it was
hopeless. For one thing, it seemed to be full of
recipes and knitting patterns. You can't read a
knitting pattern, there's no story. At least with
a recipe you can imagine eating things, and how
they'll taste. So she tried that. The trouble was, the
recipe was for chicken and mushroom casserole,
and she kept getting rhubarb in it. She discovered
that just as you can keep repeating rhubarb rhubarb
inside your head to drown out other people, you
can do it with your own thoughts.

6 oz mushrooms washed and diced

What if they don't get the baby?

1/2 pint chicken stock

What if the Boss isn't even there any
more?

Rhubarb rhubarb rhubarb
2 bay leaves
And what if he's sent for reinforce-
ments?
What if—?
Rhubarb rhubarb rhubarb
Lightly fry the chicken cubes in oil
Or what if the Boss knows I'm here, and
comes and—
Oh rhubarb rhubarb rhubarb rhubarb
Oh if only I'd never bought those plums
in the first place!

There she goes again. Ellie's head was full of
rhubarb when Plum found her at last. He was
up there in the windy darkness and his eyes were
beginning to water when he looked down through
what seemed like the millionth roof – and there
she was!

'Hurray!'

He spun his wheels and swooped down, and
next minute was in the Moons' living-room. He
left the bicycle outside, of course. Angels can go
through walls and closed doors, but bicycles are
hopeless at this.

'Ellie!'

'Plum!'

Mr Moon jumped and Mrs Moon dropped her needle.

'Where've you been?'

Mrs Moon shrieked, 'Is he here? Is that angel here?'

'Hush, Kitty, you'll scare him off!'

'The police have gone to Forest Road,' Ellie told Plum.

'I know! But they'll never find the house. There isn't a number Thirteen. Never has been. And the Boss has started the clock, and he's doing the jigsaw and—'

'*What*?'

Mrs Moon said faintly, 'I don't believe this is happening.'

'The jigsaw! And time's running out!'

'What jigsaw?'

It was hopeless. Everyone was talking at once, and two of the people there couldn't even see the other two. And all of them had only half the plot.

FIFTEEN

MR MOON TO THE RESCUE

M r Moon was very upset when he found that number Thirteen Forest Road would be invisible to the police. It seemed to go right against the spirit of Neighbourhood Watch.

'And there was me thinking we'd got the whole thing sorted.'

'I don't like the sound of that Boss man,' his wife said. 'He sounds worse than my Uncle Eric.'

The Boss was worse than anybody's Uncle Eric. He was worse than any human being could possibly be.

'Could *I* see that house?' Mr Moon addressed the thin air where Plum's voice seemed to be coming from.

Plum hesitated.

'I *think* so. The rules are terribly complicated. But you're in on this now. You can hear us. And – I wonder . . .'

'What?' Ellie asked.

'You see – my wings are growing back.'

'Oh Plum!'

Ellie looked and sure enough, they were there, little white wings poking through his sweater. They were too small for him, she could see that, and not much use for flying. It was as if a pigeon were going round with a sparrow's wings.

'So I might be able – hang on.'

They waited, wondering what he meant and what he was doing. Whatever it was was invisible, inside Plum's head. I can't tell you, because I don't know what goes on inside an angel's head. No one does.

Whatever it was, it worked. Mrs Moon let out a little shriek and her husband blinked rapidly. Only Ellie did not notice anything different. She had been able to see Plum all along.

'Oh! Oh! You're not a bit—'

Mrs Moon was going to say that Plum was not a bit as she had imagined an angel. He was seriously lacking in the snowy wings and harp and halo department.

'Bless my soul!' said Mr Moon, and meant it.

'Great! Terrific! You *can* see me! Wow! I'm getting it back! Wait!'

They did, and this time they all saw him shut his eyes and seem to concentrate very hard.

'Oh, there you are!' cried Mrs Moon. She meant Ellie, who was suddenly there in the little crowded room.

Mr Moon recognised her at once, but his wife didn't. Ellie was not in the least like Little Bo Peep or Mary Mary. Mrs Moon at once dropped her secret hope that she might adopt her. She should have known better than even think about it. Things never turn out as you imagine they will. The only way you can get a world exactly as you want it to be is to write your own story. The real world is a wild and stubborn place, and there's very little you can do to change it. Pity.

Anyway, all four of them stood there looking at one another, rather shyly. They were certainly an ill-assorted bunch. One girl with great scared eyes, one butcher built like an ox and with fingers like sausages, one woman with a knitted cardigan and birds' nest hair, and one angel who looked nothing like what anyone had ever imagined an angel to look like. Except for the wings. The wings were not much to write home about, but they were there. Definitely there.

'So now what?' Mr Moon asked. 'Does that mean things are getting better, us being able to see the pair of you? And very pleased to meet you, of course.'

'I think so, yes. Yes, it must! My wings are growing, I'm getting stronger!'

'So – can you get that baby out?' Mrs Moon needed to know this, because now she was harbouring secret hopes that perhaps she could adopt that instead.

Plum said 'No. Not on my own.'

'There are four of us,' Mr Moon said. 'Why don't we just get over there and have a go?'

'Oh *Billy*!' his wife shrieked. 'What about those men with guns?'

Ellie said, 'They can see me – they've been able to see me all along. And the police are looking for me, and now *they* might be able to see me. Can you really see me, Mr and Mrs Moon? Really?'

She noticed a mirror and ran towards it and was looking straight into her own eyes.

'Oh, thank goodness!' It was a five-star moment. Gold-plated.

Plum began to wonder whether he had done the right thing. It was true, perhaps now the police might be able to see Ellie.

'We've got to get there somehow,' he said. 'Time's running out.'

Four pairs of eyes went to the clock on the mantelpiece.

'Disguise?' suggested Ellie. 'You said you could make me look like whatever I liked.'

'That was then,' Plum told her. 'Not now you've come visible.'

In the silence that followed you could almost hear the sound of brains being racked.

'The caravan!' said Mr Moon suddenly.

'What?'

'Perfect! Already hitched up, ready for tomorrow.'

'We go to the coast Sundays, see,' Mrs Moon explained. 'Billy likes the fishing.'

'But now we've got bigger fish to fry, eh?' Mr Moon was excited. He couldn't remember ever being so excited before, not since he was a boy, anyhow. He hazily saw himself as St George facing an outsized dragon. Or Robin Hood. Or Superman.

'We don't know if the police will still be there when we get to Forest Road,' he said. 'But if they are – what'll they see? A car and a caravan. And *you*,' he looked at Ellie and Plum, 'will be safely stowed inside it!'

Mrs Moon asked 'Where will I be? Am I going?'

'Of course you are, Kitty. Safety in numbers.'

'I could have the hysterics! What if I get the hysterics?'

'You won't. Nobody will.' Mr Moon was a commander, drilling his troops. 'If it makes you feel safer, you go in the van as well.'

'Isn't it illegal? I thought you told me it was illegal to be in a caravan when it's in motion. You told me that the time we were on our way to Bangor, and I wanted to lie down a bit.'

'The law's an ass!' declared Mr Moon, throwing his Neighbourhood Watch cap to the winds. 'There's no one going to come to any harm between here and Forest Road. It's only a few hundred yards.'

'It does seem a good idea, Mr Moon,' Plum said.

He wished he had thought of it himself, or something like it. He still wasn't doing much in the guardian angel department.

'The caravan'll be our HQ,' Mr Moon said. 'Mobile Incident Room. It's what the police do, when there's a murder hunt.'

'Don't say that, Billy! There's no one been murdered and nobody going to be.'

'Course not. Just a manner of speaking.'

'Let's go!' Plum tried to take the initiative.

'Just a minute!'

Plum turned.

'You got in here,' Mr Moon said. 'How did you get in? The doors are locked.'

'Easy. Just walked through.'

'What?'

'Watch.'

Plum walked towards the closed door of the living-room and straight through it. The others gasped. He came back through again.

'Easy peasy.'

He was showing off. Angels aren't meant to, of

course. If he doesn't look out, his wings will start shrinking again.

Mr Moon said, 'I'll get the car started.'

Plum said, 'The bike. We'd better take the bike. It's by the front door.'

Mr Moon nodded.

'I'll put it in.'

'Shall I make a flask of tea? I always make a flask of tea.'

'Not now, Kitty – no time. Quick – get your coat on – it's cold out here.'

It was, too. The wind that had been blowing through the town all day now had ice on its breath. A fearful cold was streaming from that house in Forest Road. Inside, the small front room had become a vast echoing hall of ice. Its walls and floor and ceilings were like polished marble.

Now there was very little left of the floor to see. The jigsaw had been growing steadily, piece by piece. The Boss crouched over it, his blind clever fingers moving over the scattered pieces.

Tick tock went the clock.

In one corner, far away now, was the wolf-woman. She gazed hungrily down at the small white face of the sleeping baby. There was a red glint in her eyes, and from time to time her lips drew back in a wolfish grin.

Ellie Horner was almost lost. She was poised on the edge of a black hole, and would fall down and down into the terrible pit that was the Land of the Starless Night.

Sixteen

A CHANGE IN THE WEATHER

Mr Moon blew on his fingers and shivered.
'Ready?' he called softly. 'Look sharp –
it's freezing!'

Out they came and were shocked by the cold.
Ellie felt the goosebumps rise as they hurried forward
toward the waiting caravan. In the muddy light of the
streetlamps she could see their breath like smoke.

'All sit on the floor,' Mr Moon whispered.
'Safety first.'

As they did so, the radio crackled.

'Calling all units. Calling all units. Over.'

Plum held out the radio and they stared at it,
transfixed.

'Calling all units, calling all units. Over.'

'Give it here!'

Mr Moon took the radio from Plum.

'Moon here, Moon here. Over.'

There was a silence, a long silence.

'Are you receiving me? Over.'

Another silence. Then 'All units back to base. Repeat. All units back to base. Over.'

'You listen here,' Mr Moon said. 'We know your game, and we're coming after you. You hear me? Over.'

The radio crackled.

'P'raps he can't hear you,' Ellie whispered.

Then the radio spat.

'Too late! You hear me – too late!'

Mr Moon said 'You listen here. It's Moon here, Neighbourhood Watch. You put that baby outside the door, and we'll say no more about it.'

'And wrap it up well!' His wife leaned forward to speak into the mouthpiece.

'You hear me? You hear me? Over.'

The radio spluttered, but there was no answer.

'On way,' Mr Moon said. 'On way.'

He handed the radio back to Plum.

'Let's get started!'

He climbed down and shut the door behind him. The trio sat on the floor, their legs stretched in front of them, and gazed at one another with wide, frightened eyes.

'He said it was too late.' Ellie's voice was a ghost of a whisper.

Plum shook his head.

'Not true. Never is.'

The words were meant to comfort, but they did not.

Too late. Too late.

You've had it, Ellie Horner.

Goodbye, world, dear old world.

Goodbye Mum and Dad and Sam.

And I've never been to Disney World.

And I'll never be a doctor when I grow up.

I'll never grow up.

I like the world, I want to stay!

Oh, if only, if only . . .

Starless Night. It gives you the shivers.

Starless—

Rhubarb rhubarb rhubarb rhubarb

The Boss is going to get me.

Suck suck suck

Suck suck suck suck suck

Curled on the floor of the caravan, eyes shut, Ellie Horner was sucking her thumb again.

She hardly heard the car engine start. They moved forward, and the caravan was rocking, swaying as if it were at sea.

'She's never gone to sleep!'

'Scared,' Plum said. 'Scared to death.'

'Oh, bless her heart! There, little duck, there, it'll be all right!'

A hand was stroking her hair.

Mr Moon, alone in the car, saw the first snow. Tiny chipped grains spinning under the streetlamps.

'This is a rum go,' he told himself. There was no one else to tell.

He drove on steadily. The flakes grew bigger. Soon they were tossing in the wind like torn tissue. The road ahead was white. He turned on the screen wipers and peered forward. The headlamps of an oncoming car showed like the eyes of a huge owl.

Mr Moon hardly knew what he was doing here. Why he was driving his car at almost midnight. Why he was towing a caravan containing (illegally) two people and an angel with very small wings. He didn't really have a plan. He meant to burst straight into the house in Forest Road and snatch the baby.

He knew about the Boss and the wolf-woman. He had been told about the giant jigsaw and the ticking clock. But grown-ups are scared of different things from children. Grown-ups are scared of losing their jobs, or getting behind with the rent. Things like that. They hardly ever think about really scary things. Most of them have forgotten that they were once frightened of the dark, and that the world seemed a dangerous and haunted place.

Even now, in a September snowstorm at nearly midnight, Mr Moon didn't spend much time wondering what on earth he was getting into. He thought fleetingly that there wasn't much chance of getting to the coast tomorrow, not with this weather. Mostly he concentrated on the road, white over now and treacherous. He slowed to a crawl, changing carefully down through the gears. At that moment he was more worried about the police than the Boss.

The word goes round about the town that it is snowing, snowing in September. Most of the children and most families are in bed and fast asleep. But there are always more people about at midnight than you think. People on their way home from parties, or coming off a shift. People walking their dogs, or letting the cat out. People who can't sleep, and lie wide-eyed in a dark, shrunken world of their own. From time to time they get up and flick on the light, or look out of the window, to reassure themselves that the real world is still there.

At Ellie's house, Sam is already asleep, though he has missed his sister's goodnight kiss, and the rhymes she sometimes sings. Mr and Mrs Horner sit opposite one another, waiting for the phone to ring. From time to time Mrs Horner gets up, goes to the window and lifts a corner of the curtain to look out. That is when she sees the snow. She lets out a shriek that brings her husband over, and the pair stare out in disbelief. Their beloved daughter has gone missing and there is snow in September. The whole world has gone upside down.

It is the cats who hate the snow most. All day the wind has been blowing their fur the wrong way, and now their whiskers are wet, and their paws. They spit and growl deep in their throats. They give up the night's hunting and make for sheds and porches or their own flaps. Hunched and furious they spit and growl and glare into the foreign whiteness. The night is their territory, and it is being stolen from them. Some of the fiercest brave the snow and head for Forest Road. They know there are aliens there, have known all day. Silently they assemble on the pavement outside number Thirteen, fur bristling, eyes fixed murderously on the dimly lit window.

In the vast, icy hall that had been the front room of number Thirteen, the jigsaw is almost completed. The Boss is steadily slotting in the remaining pieces. Click click.

The wolf-woman towers and gloats over the baby. She opens her eyes and gazes up at her, as mild and trusting as if she is looking at her own mother.

The old clock is ticking and the echoes run about the gleaming walls. The air is dense with ticking. The fingers stand at four minutes to twelve.

'Rock a bye baby on the tree top
When the wind blows the cradle will rock.'

The wolf-woman is chanting in a hoarse, tuneless voice. Her red eyes glint as they meet the baby's gaze.

'When the bough breaks the cradle will fall
Down will come baby, cradle and all.'

The baby seems to know the song, if not the voice, and smiles.

Seventeen

THE BOSS PLAYS HIS TRUMP

The snow kept coming, but it never occurred to Mr Moon to turn back. He had started something that he meant to finish. His very soul rebelled against the idea of babies being stolen, children hunted, shots fired in his own town. He was ready for a fight.

At last he turned carefully into Forest Road and saw with enormous relief that the police were not there. The only fear he had was that he would be caught by them with his illegal cargo. There were no tall men with pulled-down hats and belted coats, either, unless they were farther down, veiled by the thickly falling snow. The whole thing began to look like a piece of cake.

He peered at his watch. Three minutes to twelve. More haste less speed, he told himself, as his heart began to thud. He crawled along the kerb, counting numbers. When he saw the army of cats ahead he guessed he had reached his destination. Braking gently he brought the car to a halt and switched off the engine.

As he climbed out, Plum already had the door of the caravan open and was dancing up and down, shivering. Ellie followed slowly, like a sleepwalker, and last came Mrs Moon, pop-eyed with the strangeness of it all. She saw the cats and stiffened. The police she had half-expected, but not this offbeat nursery rhyme scenario.

'Hark hark the dogs do bark

The beggars are coming to town.'

The lines came into Ellie's head as she gazed fearfully at the door of the narrow house. Number Thirteen. The house the neighbours could not see, or the police.

Mr Moon scrunched purposefully towards it, scattering the cats. He banged hard on the door.

'Moon here! Open up!'

The four of them waited, hugging themselves and shivering with more than cold. Again Mr Moon banged.

'Open up, or I'm coming in!'

Silence. The silence of snow.

Mr Moon was not a fan of *The Bill* for nothing. He motioned the others to stand aside, and himself fell back a few paces. He drew a deep breath, then ran and kicked at the door with all his force, just as he had so often seen his heroes do on the screen. It flew open.

All four stood pole-axed as they saw what lay beyond. No crowded room with sofas, chairs, rugs, but a great bare gleaming hall. They were standing on the threshold of another world. They stared, stunned, as if they would stand like that forever.

It was the loud tick of the clock that brought them back to their senses. That, and the growling and spitting of the cats. They could see the figure of a man at an immense distance, kneeling, slotting in pieces of the jigsaw that they now saw stretched the whole great width and length of the room. Of the baby and the wolf-woman there was no sign.

'Pass that baby over!' Mr Moon's voice was stern and loud.

The Boss did not even look up. He had no time to waste on words. he was only a few pieces away from midnight. The Ellie-shaped hole in the world was soon to be filled.

Mr Moon's eyes went to the clock, and then he too knew that words were useless. This was it.

'Here I come!'

He was over the threshold and looking about him, and then he did see the wolf-woman, crouching in the farthest corner behind the door. She bared her teeth and snatched up a bundle from a basket and hugged it fiercely to her. A baby began to cry.

'There goes your jigsaw! To hell with your jigsaw! There! There! There!'

He is in there, kicking left and right. Pieces of jigsaw fly up about him. There are howls from the wolf-woman and the Boss lets out a scream of fury as his whole day's painstaking work is undone in seconds.

'Stop! I warn you – stop!'

But Mr Moon isn't listening, he's kicking his way through the jigsaw to the corner where the wolf-woman is cowering.

Go for it, Billy Moon, go for it! You're on a mission, you're nearly there!

Now he can see the wolf-woman clearly, her bared teeth and eyes glinting red.

Mrs Moon screams 'Billy! Billy! Be careful!' and without realising it, she too steps forward into the icy hall and can see the distant wolf-woman and the baby. Ellie follows her, and doesn't notice that Plum is hanging back on the doorstep, with the swarming cats. They have met an invisible barrier, and cannot follow.

Plum sees that the Boss is getting to his feet, and wonders fearfully what other secret weapons he might have.

The Boss is making fast for the clock, and seems not to care that now he too is trampling on his precious jigsaw. Mrs Moon thinks he is making for her husband, and screams again.

'Billy! Billy! Look out!'

The Boss reaches the clock, and stops it. There is sudden, total silence, the silence of vacuum.

The Boss has stopped the clock. Time is standing still.

The Boss may be king of the Land of the Starless Night, but his power does not end there. Beyond his foothold in Forest Road the whole town is now in his thrall.

The cats on the pavement outside are frozen, their mouths open in mid-yowl, their eyes fixed in glassy stares. The snow stops. The flakes that are already falling drift and settle, and then there are no more. Suddenly there is a sky again, a huge, starry sky.

If you could travel through that town, not only its streets and squares, but its houses too, you would know that you were in the land of the Sleeping Beauty. And such is the silence that you would think that the spell could easily last for a hundred years.

See how quietly the children sleep in their beds. They lie like effigies. Blankets and quilts are neat and flat. In the next room their parents lie in the same unnatural peace.

Sam is motionless in his bed among his toys. Downstairs, Mr and Mrs Horner stare wide-eyed across the room at one another, and a huge question mark still hangs in the air between them.

Throughout the town police cars stand locked in freeze-frame. The streets are littered with them. A drunk stands, head tilted, a can to his lips, and a man and his dog are sculpted, one in mid-stride, the other with leg cocked against a lamppost.

Even the pigeons and starlings in their roosts are like stone birds with lidded eyes on the whitened roofs under the moon. Because the moon is back, and the snow gleams under a cold lunatic light. It falls on the motionless cats and dogs and people like limelight in a theatre.

But wait. If you were Plum, and could go up above the trees and roofs and chimney pots and look down on the spellbound town, you would see movements. You would see tall figures going in pairs. They stream out of the large square building behind the precinct, then strike out again in different directions.

The hunt is on again.

EIGHTEEN

WINGS

The only people who are not frozen in time are Ellie and Plum, Billy and Kitty Moon. They still do not realise that time has stopped, though they guess that the boss has stopped the clock for a reason. They are right.

The Boss has a plan to fall back on in an emergency. He nods to the wolf-woman, who starts to move. Over the jigsaw she goes with long strides, still fiercely clutching the baby. She goes past the Boss, who feels the icy draught as she goes, though he does not see her.

Mr Moon has smartly placed himself between her and the open door. But she is not making for that. She is heading towards another door at the far end of the great hall.

'She's going out the back! After her!' Mr Moon's bellow strikes echoes, they ricochet about the room.

'Stop!' The Boss raises a hand. 'I warn you! Let her go!'

Something about the blind eyes in the waxen face makes Mr Moon pause.

'Death! If you go after her you are going to your own death!'

The words are spoken softly and the echoes a mere hissing over the polished ice.

Mr Moon hesitates for only a fraction of a second. Then he plunges onward, spurting up a trail of jigsaw pieces.

Mrs Moon screams 'Billy!'

Plum looks down and sees the cats with frozen snarls and glassy eyes, and guesses what the Boss has done.

At present he does not know why. To buy time, of course, time to reassemble the broken jigsaw. But now the baby has gone, the wolf-woman is heading back to the outside world. What's his game?

Plum does not know that the tall men with guns are streaming out of the police station in the town. He does not know that they are already splitting into pairs, striking off in different directions, combing the white streets. The wolf-woman is being used as a decoy.

The Boss knows. He smiles a slow blind smile, falls to his knees and begins the work of mending his broken jigsaw. Ellie and Mrs Moon watch him, mesmerised.

Plum calls, 'Ellie, come on! Mrs Moon!' They turn. 'We've got to go after her! The baby!'

They seem to hear that last word and respond. They hurry over and are back in the snowy street. Ellie sees the cats, stiff and staring, and gasps.

'What—?'

'Time! He's stopped time!'

'*What*?'

'We've got them now! She's out here and there are four of us against one! Quick!'

Mrs Moon said 'But – I can't go very fast! Oh, that poor baby! Not in all this snow!'

Plum already has the bicycle and is wheeling it back towards the High Street. The other two stumble after him, trying to keep up.

'P'raps Mr Moon's already got her!

★   ★   ★

161

He is wrong. The wolf-woman's strides are long and swift. Mr Moon's hobby is fishing, not cross-country running. He can still see her ahead, but is losing ground.

If she goes out of sight I can follow her tracks, he thinks. She'll think she's thrown me off, but she'll be wrong. Oh no. I shan't give up. Not Billy Moon.

His eyes go automatically down and that is when he notices. The wolf-woman is speeding down a narrow alley into a back street, and he follows her. There are no prints in the snow. He can't believe his eyes. He swiftly checks behind him. There are his own blurred tracks, but no sign that the wolf-woman has passed the same way.

This is a nasty shock. It gives Billy Moon some idea of what he is getting into. Even now he has only half the story. He has handed the radio back to Plum, and it is Plum, two streets away, who hears the Boss's voice.

'Calling all units. Calling all units. They're on the street, the boy and the girl. They just left. And there's a man called Moon and his wife – you'll spot them easily. Shoot on sight. Repeat. Shoot on sight.'

Ellie and Mrs Moon have heard this too. They stare, appalled, at the small black radio that has pronounced their death sentence.

'Who – who's he talking to?' Mrs Moon asks at last.

'His men,' Plum tells her. 'Looks as if they're on the loose again. At least we've been warned.'

Ellie cries, 'But they're on their way! They must be now!'

'So we find that baby – fast!' he tells her. 'Come on – we'll have to go up!'

He pushes the bicycle over to Ellie.

'Go on! Get on!'

'But—'

'Do it!'

She obeys.

Mrs Moon says, 'What about me? What shall I do?'

'Keep going,' Plum tells her. 'If you see the men – freeze. The only way they'll spot you is if you're moving!'

Ellie and Mrs Moon both look and see the man and his dog in freeze-frame. They are eerily lit by the streetlamp above and are poised in a huge unearthly silence. The whole world is holding its breath.

'Go on!' Plum tells Ellie. She is astride the bicycle now, though she doesn't know why. 'Go!'

She screams, 'I can't ride it in all this snow! *You* ride it – if you go up you'll see her!'

'We're both going up.'

'*What*?'

'Look at my wings!'

She looks and sees that they have grown. They are suddenly there, strong and white and bristling. Now at last, even in sweatshirt and jeans, Plum looks like a proper angel.

'Oooh I never! Oooh I never!' says Mrs Moon faintly. The world has gone mad. Her town is littered with human statues and men with guns, and now angels.

'Go!' Plum orders again.

Ellie is shuddering and her teeth are chattering. She hardly knows what she is doing, or why. Her head won't work.

It's all gone wrong.

Everything's gone pear-shaped.

Plum's got wings, real wings.

Whacking great big wings.

But oh – she's gone and taken the baby!

And the men with guns are back.

Rhubarb rhubarb rhubarb

We'll never get that baby back, never!

He's stopped time.

The world isn't working any more.

Oh Mum, Dad, where are you!

I don't like it, I don't like it I don't—

Wheeeeee!

She hardly knows it, but she has started pedalling and Plum is pushing her and the front wheel is tilting upward. There is a sudden strong thrust as if the bicycle has come alive and—

'Lift off!'

She hears Plum's yell and looks to see that he is airborne, and only a wing's span away. That is when she realises that she is, too.

She looks down. She is already way above the rooftops and below she can see Mrs Moon and the man and his dog in a pool of light. Faintly she hears Mrs Moon's voice.

'Oh! Oh! Come back! Come back!'

But Ellie won't come back – can't. The bicycle has taken on a mysterious power of its own. She is living a dream, biking it over the roofs and chimney pots in great sweeping arcs. The only sounds are the hiss of her wheels and nearby the beat of Plum's wings. They are lords of the sky up there, and the moon seems only a fingertip away, so near and real that a cow could jump over it.

'Yahoo!' comes Plum's triumphant shout. 'Yahoo – we've done it!'

NINETEEN

THE ELLIE-SHAPED HOLE

In the streets below, the wolf-woman is still striding, striding, and Mr Moon goes after her, desperate and out of puff. He stops for a moment to catch his breath and sees a police car parked nearby. There is a blue light but it does not flash.

'Gotcha!' he gasps, and staggers over. Soon every squad car in town will be on red alert.

But the car is not parked. It is in mid-road where it has stopped at a minute before twelve. Inside are two officers. They sit like waxworks, eyes set on the traffic lights ahead that show amber, and will show amber until the clocks are started again.

Mr Moon does not know that time is standing still. He bangs on the window of the car.

'You! What's the matter with you! Here!'

The policemen's faces are calm and blank. Their eyes don't blink. They are maddening, impossible.

Mr Moon furiously kicks the side of the car and stumbles off, but the wolf-woman is out of sight. He has lost her, and she leaves no tracks.

It'll be gone midnight now, all right, he thinks. But we've still got time. He's got to put that jigsaw together again. I know – 999!

He scans about and sees a house with a downstairs light still on. If ever there was a time for Neighbourhood Watch, this is it. He hammers on the door.

'Open up! Help! Moon here, Neighbourhood Watch! Open up!'

Behind the curtains a man is sitting with his hand in a bag of crisps. He is staring at a screen that shows men playing football, though they do not move. They are poised in action, like the figures in a Find the Ball photograph.

Mr Moon bangs and hammers and shouts. He doesn't care if he rouses the whole street (though there is no fear of that).

'What's the *matter* with 'em!'

He whirls about, spots another lighted window farther down the road and makes for it.

In a nearby side alley (the town is full of them)

the wolf-woman crouches and bares her teeth in a grin. She has the baby pressed hard against her to stifle her cries. She watches the retreating figure and grins again. The game is a good one and it is going well.

Mr Moon does not know that at any moment he may meet a pair of tall men with guns. His wife does. She cranes to watch Plum and Ellie in the sky and tells herself over and over again that she is dreaming. The pair duck and dive among the trees and chimney pots and then they have gone.

She can feel the wet snow on her slippered feet. Back to earth, she gazes fearfully at the man and his dog, and feels the unearthly silence. She has never felt so alone in her life. She knows that she will not be much help in chasing the wolf-woman. The thought occurs to her that she can go home and put the kettle on. Everyone will be ready for a nice cup of tea when this is all over. She could even warm some soup.

Nodding to herself she sets off, planting her feet carefully as if she were on stepping stones. Once she is safely home the world will come to rights, she knows it. Her crowded little sitting-room will still be there with its treasures, the kettle will boil, the gas fire flicker. She can even sit and sew her squirrel while she waits.

She reaches the end of Forest Road and turns the corner. There, right in front of her, is a police car! She waves her arms and calls. (She has already forgotten that time is standing still, even if she believed it in the first place. Time does not stand still. It never has.)

She can see two policemen in the car but they do not seem to see her. She flaps over the snow, careless of her slippers, and sees them both looking straight ahead, unwinking as dummies. She taps on the window. They do not turn their heads.

'Wake up! Wake up!' she screams.

This is a mistake. A pair of tall men are advancing up a side street opposite. They nod to one another and hurry their steps. Their hands go to their pockets and their guns.

Plum and Ellie are scanning the network of streets and alleys that run behind Forest Road. Now they are lit by the moon as well as lamps, and are bleak and bare and white. Nothing moves. The pair go wordlessly, hunting like owls. Sooner or later the wolf-woman must break her cover and then they have her. They will swoop down and snatch the baby from her arms, and the Ellie-shaped hole in the world will be filled again.

All the while Ellie is thinking I'm flying, I'm flying! She half-hopes she might stop like this forever and make a nest among the stars. She forgets about the lost baby that is really herself, and goes into steep dives and wheelings like a young bird trying its wings.

All at once the air below her is peppered with orange sparks.

Crack! Crack! Crack!

She screams and swallows a bucketful of air. At first she doesn't see Plum. She has gone high, higher than ever she meant to – even forgotten what she was meant to be doing.

Plum hasn't. For him, everything depends on it. He spots the wolf-woman as she breaks cover. She darts from an alley, hoping to escape under the covering fire of the tall men. But Plum is a proper angel again now – a guardian angel and afraid of nothing.

As Ellie screams she sees the wolf-woman, but only for a split second before a pair of white wings goes over her in a hail of orange darts.

'Plum! Plum!'

She goes into a nose dive but sees that Plum has snatched the baby from the wolf-woman's arms and is already beating upward, as if to meet her in mid-sky.

Then things happen so fast that afterwards she can never quite remember, and even wonders if she dreamed it all. There is a long slow yawn of light, a bright yellowness that roofs the whole town with gold. At the same time there is a great triumphant sound that is like cocks crowing, trumpets, bells and children cheering all at once.

Ellie is dazzled and deafened. Nothing like this has ever happened before. She looks down and the whole town seems to be moving as if there is an earthquake. Then she guesses.

The whole world is going into a gigantic shuffle, while the Ellie-shaped hole in it is being filled again. She's back in the world, but never dreamed that she could have made such a difference. At least as much difference as a butterfly flapping its wings

in a steamy rainforest. As much difference as me
– or you.

Me, she thinks. It's all because of me. Out loud
she yells, 'We did it! We did it! Plum!'

She calls the last word urgently, because Plum
is going up and past her with a steady beat of
wings. In his arms she glimpses the baby, a little
white-faced thing, the cause of all the trouble.

'Plum!' she screams.

He is going higher and past her. She looks upward
to follow his progress and has to shade her eyes
with her hand because of the stars' winking and
blinking.

She doesn't realise at first that the bicycle is
going down. She cranes and stares to catch her
last glimpse of Plum and his wings going in and
out like scissors. This is it! All at once she knows
that she will never see him again, and never
properly see the baby that is her own self. Again
she cries 'Plum! Plum!' because she doesn't want
the story to end.

But she feels the plummeting of the bike and
looks away just in time to see that she is level with
the church steeple. Down she goes willy-nilly and

her feet have barely touched the ground when the clock begins to strike.

The Ellie-shaped hole in the world has been filled again and the town settles. Children stir and mutter in their beds. The roosting pigeons in the precinct hunch dreamlessly on their ledges.

Ellie is home again, really home now, and the well-known chimes are telling the hour. It is midnight. All stories must have an end, and midnight is as good a time as any.

AFTERWARDS

Fairy stories usually end with 'And they all lived happily ever after.' We never get to know the details. This isn't a fairy tale, it's a slice of life, and in real life nobody lives happily ever after, only happily some of the time ever after.

So it's goodbye Ellie, goodbye Plum. We can only wonder what Ellie said to her mother and father when she burst through the door at midnight. And what Mr and Mrs Moon said to one another afterwards. And who knows what the police made of it all. Did they even remember? The tall men had left no trace. There had been no wallets or keys or photos when they were taken into custody and told to empty their pockets. And when they had walked out just before midnight they had picked up their guns and radios as they went.

As for Thirteen Forest Road, it had never existed. Nothing to check on there, no clues – not even the odd piece of jigsaw. The Boss must have furiously crammed the pieces into their bags and hoofed it as fast as he could, back to the Land of the Starless Night. And the wolf-woman must have skedaddled there pronto. And the men in hats and raincoats.

Where that is we don't know, and I for one don't wish to find out. But there's one thing for sure. If what Plum said is true, we're all on the Boss's list, so we'd better look out.

Ellie probably never saw Plum again. But she didn't ever wonder if the whole thing had really happened at all, or whether she had imagined it. She had only to go to the library and sit on the seat and gaze up into the branches of a young oak.

And there were plenty of questions asked about *that*.